<- Item Banner ->

THE TEN
SLEEP MURDERS

The Ten Sleep Murders

BILLY HALL

A Black Horse Western

ROBERT HALE · LONDON

ISBN 0 7090 5867 5

Robert Hale Limited
Clerkenwell House
Clerkenwell Green
London EC1R 0HT

Photoset in North Wales by
Derek Doyle & Associates, Mold, Clwyd.
Printed and bound in Great Britain by
WBC Book Manufacturers Limited,
Bridgend, Mid-Glamorgan.

ONE

Death hung in the still air. Levi could taste it. He could feel it. Like the tickling feet of a spider, it crawled up his spine. He could taste it in the salt of his sweat, as he licked his lips.

From long experience he knew enough to be still. Watch. Wait. The man on the ground needed no haste. It was obvious he was dead. His horse stood patiently, reins dragging the ground. He waited for a master who would never ride again.

The dead man lay in a twisted heap where he had fallen. One leg jutted awkwardly to one side. The other was twisted beneath him. His hat lay several feet to one side, exposing sandy-coloured hair, slightly grey at the temples. The gaping hole where a bullet had exited his back, carrying bone fragments and life with it, left no doubt he was dead.

Levi watched cautiously through the clump of sage. He was hunkered down below the rim of a small gully. Only his head, from the eyes up, was exposed, even that only through the screening of the brush.

A deer fly buzzed close around his head. He resisted the urge to swat at it, holding perfectly still. A small swarm of gnats buzzed in front of his face. It was so still he could almost hear the buzzing of their wings. A trickle of sweat crossed the mark where his hat usually rode. It traced a slow course down across his face.

He squinted over his shoulder at the Wyoming sun, near to setting behind the Absaroka Mountains. Another hour to dark. His horse munched grass about fifty feet behind him, hidden at the bottom of the ravine. Levi glanced around at him occasionally. He knew the horse's keener hearing would detect anyone's approach before his own ears would. There was no such indication.

Finally, slowly and silently, he slid backward from his vantage point. He replaced his Stetson. Still gripping the Winchester .44-40 carbine, he began to creep along the gully toward the place he guessed the shot had come from.

Long practice made him instinctively aware of the distance from the shot. He crept about 500 yards up the gully, then crawled to the top of a low hillock. He again screened himself carefully with brush. When he moved, he made no noise. His caution blended him into the terrain like a silent shadow. Below him he spotted the trampled grass where the dry-gulcher had waited with deadly purpose. There was nobody there now.

He stood and walked the thirty yards or so to the place from which the shot was fired. He carefully searched the area, foot by foot. He finished as the sun tossed its last efforts at daylight across the valley.

Levi frowned as he returned to his horse. There were few tracks left at the site. Those whispers of track indicated a small man, but there was not one single clearly defined track to identify him. Neither was there spent brass from the cartridge. Either the killer had left without reloading, or had taken care to take the expended brass with him.

'Either he was danged awful sure of himself or mighty careful,' he observed to himself. 'Either one means somebody cool as a crick bottom.'

Retrieving his horse, he finally turned his attention to the dead man. He had a couple of gold coins in his pocket. There was a good cattleman's three-bladed pocket knife; a small piece of rock looked like it might be gold ore. A few wooden matches finished the contents of his pants pockets. His shirt pocket held only a bag of Bull Durham tobacco and a package of cigarette papers.

It was the Bull Durham package that caused Levi to stare, scowling. The round tag on the end of the pull strings was always left hanging out of a man's pocket. The killer had used it for a target, putting a .30 hole in its exact centre from almost 300 yards.

'That feller's some kind of shot,' he muttered, looking over his shoulder for the tenth time. 'Looks like I'm up against a real pro this time.'

Levi hoisted the man's body on to his horse, tying him into place with the man's own lariat. That done, he remounted his own horse.

'Well, Smoky,' he addressed his horse, 'guess we'll ride late tonight. I ain't in the mood to sleep with a corpse. We'll try to ride on into Ten Sleep 'stead o' campin' another night.'

It was nearly midnight when he rode into Ten Sleep with his grisly cargo and found the marshal's office. Dismounting, he knocked quietly.

'Who's there?' a deep voice rumbled softly.

'Name's Levi Hill,' Levi answered just as softly. 'Outa Cheyenne. You Marshal Hansen?'

'Uh huh. You the investigator?'

'Yup.'

'Always come along in the middle of the night?'

Levi chuckled in spite of himself. 'Naw, just when I feel the itch to get some marshal outa bed.' He waited for just a couple of heartbeats, then continued, 'Actually, I found what looks like another murder on the way. I didn't want to lay out another night with a dead man for company, so I brung him on in.'

There was silence for a full minute, then the glow of a kerosene lantern shone under the door. The bar slid noisily from its brackets and the door opened to disclose a large man holding a Navy Colt .45 in one hand and lantern in the other.

His pale-blue eyes sized Levi up carefully, then went to the loaded horse behind him.

'Know who he is?'

'Nope. No identification on him. Figured you'd probably know him.'

'How'd he get it?'

'Bushwhacked. Shot through the chest from almost three hundred yards. Thirty-thirty, looks like. Shot his Bull Durham tag dead centre.'

The marshal grunted. 'Don't fit the pattern, but then there ain't been no pattern to fit.'

As he talked, the marshal walked into the

street. He held the lantern close to the dead man and grabbed him by the hair, lifting his head so he could see his face. He swore angrily.

'Now why'd anyone want to shoot Wade?'

'I figured he'd be someone you knew.'

'Sure, I know him. Wade Renfro. He's the foreman on the Rafter-D. He was a fine man.'

'Have a family?'

'Naw, he's a bachelor. Fine cowman. Didn't have an enemy in the world that I knowed of.'

'Somebody he fired, maybe? You said he's the Rafter-D's foreman.'

'Oh, could be, I suppose. Not likely, though. A man who gets fired may try to whip the foreman that fired him, but not likely bushwhack him.'

'Well, I guess you can take care of him. I'm going to put up my horse and see if there's a room at the hotel. I'll be over to talk in the morning.'

Without waiting for an answer, Levi took up his horse's reins and stepped back into the saddle. He turned down the street to where he had already spotted the lantern of the livery stable. He dismounted there and walked in softly. Finding an empty stall, he removed the saddle and bridle. He forked the horse some hay, pumped a bucket of water for his water trough, then picked up his saddle-bags and bedroll and walked out. The livery man would find him there in the morning. That'd be time enough to pay for his keep.

Entering the hotel he bumped the desk to wake the night clerk sleeping in his chair. The clerk never moved from the chair, only opened his eyes and spoke. 'Just sign the book and take a key. Number four faces the street. Five faces back.

Room's a dollar.'

'How much a week?'

'Four dollars.'

'Let's call it a week then. I'll take the one facing the street.'

He signed his name and walked up the creaking steps. He heard the night clerk resume his snoring almost immediately.

He found his room, and lighted the lamp in the sconce by the door. The faint glow of the light revealed a sagging bed and a dilapidated dresser. There was a wash stand, with a basin and pitcher. The mirror was cracked, and almost clean. Levi grunted and shut the door, wedging the straight-backed chair under the door knob for security. He leaned his rifle against the wall, but hung his gun-belt on the head of the bed where it would be near at hand. He pulled off his boots, and laid down on top of the covers. He was asleep almost before his head hit the pillow.

TWO

The first rays of the morning sun were hurrying toward his window when Levi wakened. He went directly to the marshal's office.

'Up bright and early for a late night,' the marshal observed.

'Figured you'd be in a hurry to get started,' Levi answered, 'especially if these fellers gettin' killed are the ones that voted for you.'

'Ain't nobody gonna vote for me if I don't get these killin's stopped,' the marshal returned dryly. 'C'mon in and we'll jaw a while.'

Inside, Levi looked around approvingly. 'You keep a clean jail,' he observed.

'Aw, it don't take much,' the marshal shrugged, ''specially if I got prisoners to help with the scrubbing.'

'Why'd you send for an investigator?' Levi asked, avoiding any further waste of time.

'Get right to it, don't you?' the marshal responded. 'Well, I guess we'd just as well. How much do you already know?'

'Just assume I don't know anything,' Levi answered. 'I'd like to hear everything you can tell me, just in case something got missed when the office filled me in.'

'Sounds reasonable. OK. Well, about six months ago there was a homesteader up along Ten Sleep Crick that got his throat slit. Then....'

Levi interrupted. 'Let's don't leave him just yet. I'd like to get as full a picture of each one as I can before we go on to the next one. That was the one named Binder?'

'That's the one. Matt Binder. He had a homestead, like I said. He was about thirty-five. Bachelor. Clean, hard-working sort. Never in any trouble that I knowed of. Didn't drink hardly at all. Went to church whenever he was in town or could. Just about proved up on his homestead. No enemies at all, far as anybody knowed.'

'Killed at home?'

'Yup. Dangdest thing I ever seen. He was sittin' at his kitchen table, with his head tipped back, but it was cut almost half off. It looked like someone slipped up behind him and just cut his throat.'

'No signs of a fight?'

'Nary a one. Nothin' out of place. Nothin' stolen as far as anybody could tell. Didn't have nothin' to steal, for that matter.'

'Sounds like something a renegade Indian might do. Been any around that you know of?'

'Nope. Couldn't been an Indian noways. Matt's pa was killed by Indians some years ago, and he hadn't no use for 'em. There ain't no way he'd let an Indian into the house, let alone behind him, an' him a-sittin' down.'

A cloud passed across Levi's face at the words. He took a deep breath, pulling himself forcibly away from memories of his own past. 'What if there were two, and one had a gun on him?'

The marshal shook his head. 'If they was Indians, they was ridin' shod horses. I'd a' noticed any unshod tracks, sure.'

'OK. Let's go on. Who was next?'

'Well, next one was about three weeks later. That was Walt McClatchey. He was a family man, owned his own ranch. The Bar-X-Bar. He was out on his own land, checking his cows. His crew was off over on the other side of the ranch. He was shot, real close up, with a forty-four or forty-five, couldn't be sure. Gun was so close it burned a big ol' spot on his shirt.'

'Shot while he was on his horse?'

'No. Funny thing. It looked like he was standin' on the ground, away from his horse. We could see where the horse jumped and run a' ways when the shot went off. It looked like he was talkin' to somebody he knowed, or at least somebody he wasn't afraid of.'

'Any tracks there?'

'No track at all, except Walt's. Most of his were gone too.'

'Gone?'

'Wiped out. Whoever did it, did a first-rate job wiping out every single track. I took Dusty Rowley out there with me. He's about the best tracker in these parts. He found where the tracks had been wiped out all the way to some rocky ground, and we never could find where the tracks left the rocky ground. He said it was the best job of track erasing he'd seen done by anyone but Indians.'

'Indians again.'

'Well, could be, I suppose. But I can't see Walt lettin' an Indian that close to him either.'

'Unless another one had a gun on him,' Levi said again.

'You sure stick to an idea, don't you?' the marshal complained.

'Just like to explore the options. Who was next?'

'Winston Caulder. Win, everyone called him. Matched his name. If we had a rodeo, he won everything he entered. If there was a card game, he won. He was honest, but he was just about the luckiest man I ever seen. He was one of those guys that does everything just a little easier and a little better than anyone else, and never even seems to work at it. You know the kind. Seemed like he just couldn't lose, no matter what he did. Till he got shot, that is.'

'Where'd he get killed?'

'Across the street. He came out of the saloon one night – been playing poker and drinkin' some. He came out front, rolled a smoke, and got shot.'

'He'd been winning again?'

'Oh, sure. He always won. Nothin' big, though. And the hands he won the money from were all still in the saloon tryin' to win some of it back from each other. It wasn't no sore loser.'

'What was he shot with?'

'Small bore rifle. Maybe about a thirty-two. Shot from between the hotel and the mercantile store. 'Bout fifty yards or less.'

'Anyone hear a horse ride away?'

'Nobody heard nothin' but the shot. Half the town heard the shot and come a-runnin', but nobody heard or seen nothin' after it. It was just like some crazy Indian snuck into town and killed him, then snuck out again.'

'Indians again. You said it this time.'

The marshal threw up his hands. 'Aw, there ain't no way no Indian's gonna come right into town and shoot someone, even if there was any around! I sent to the Cattlemen's Association for a range detective, not for somebody who sees Indians standin' over every dead body in Wyoming!'

Levi chuckled, but his eyes stayed flat and hard. 'Get kinda touchy, don't you? Who was next?'

'Well, the next was the one that made me decide to holler for some help. It was Bill Murphy. He was a homesteader, down on the Wind River. Had a wife and four of the finest kids you ever seen. He was a solid homesteader. Nearly had his place proved up. He'd a' dropped everything anytime to help anyone that needed help. He was just a fine, fine man.'

'How'd he get killed?'

'He was found drug half to pieces, with his foot hung up in his stirrup.'

'That happens. What makes you think it was murder?'

'I looked that body over real careful. He had a big hole caved in on the back of his head. That killed him. All the beatin'-up that bein' drug caused, came after he was dead. You know, a wound just looks different, when it happens after a man's already dead. All the bleedin' he did, he did out that hole in the back of his head. Somebody hit him in the head and killed him, then stuck his foot in the stirrup to make it look like an accident.'

'Was his horse spooky enough to drag him?'

'Naw! That horse was one his kids rode part of the time. That's the second thing that convinced me it was murder. They was a big ol' cockleburr jammed under the horse's tail. Whoever stuck his foot in the stirrup made real sure the horse would drag him plenty far.'

'Do you think it's connected to the rest of the murders?'

'Well of course I think so. What makes you ask?'

'It's the only one the killer tried to make look like an accident,' Levi replied.

'Yeah, but before that one, nothin' had been said about gettin' an outsider to investigate them. I figger the killer got a little scared at that idea, and decided to try makin' that one look accidental.'

Levi pursed his lips thoughtfully. 'Possible. On the other hand, there sure wasn't any effort to make the one yesterday look like an accident. It was an open murder, done by someone with practice.'

They discussed the entire situation at length, then Levi stood up to leave. The marshal said, 'Sheriff Winslow over at Worland left a badge here for you. He said to tell you you're already deputized in Washakie County, or will be, as soon as I swear you in. If you wouldn't mind a suggestion, though, it might be wise not to let folks know who you are or why you're here.'

'I thought about that some,' Levi answered, 'but it usually works better for me to just be who I am. Something about having a range detective pokin' around that tends to make people nervous. Nervous folks tend to make mistakes. 'Sides, if anyone knows somethin', they're more apt to tell me if they know I'm investigating.'

'It's your party. Ride careful.'

Levi smiled faintly. The dry smile reflected the harsh reality of a life spent as an isolated target. That life forced him to constant vigilance. 'That's kind of a habit by now.'

Maybe it was that habit that kept him uneasy as he rode out of Ten Sleep. Icy fingers squeezed his stomach. He looked around continually. Twice he grabbed his gun, without even knowing why.

'Maybe it's just the noise,' he muttered to himself.

Ten Sleep Creek was a loud, turbulent mountain stream. It teemed with trout as it rushed down Powder River Pass between Ten Sleep and Buffalo. Numerous small streams fed into it, rushing out of verdant valleys nestled between towering peaks. There was a ranch located in nearly every one of those valleys. Homesteads clung here and there, wherever the land was flat enough for hopes to grow. Those with farming in their blood saw corn and wheat sprouting on every flat piece of ground. Some starved nearly to death before they learned the Wyoming mountains were just not farmland.

When Meadowlark Creek flowed into Ten Sleep Creek he followed it, turning south along its quieter and slower flow. About an hour later he came to a solidly built homestead. For the fifth time that day, he slipped the thong from the hammer of his revolver. It was no benefit. He had no chance to even reach for it.

'Far enough, stranger!' a voice barked from the corner of the house. 'Stop right there and keep your hands where I can see 'em real good.'

Stopping his horse, Levi sized up the man who had just stepped around the corner of the house. He was unshaven, dirty, and surly looking. He was holding a double-barrelled Greener shot-gun pointed squarely at Levi's belt buckle.

'Who are you and what do you want?' the man demanded.

'Name's Levi Hill,' Levi responded, speaking with a measured, pleasant voice. 'I'm a range detective. I been hired to try to get to the bottom of the killings around here.'

'Whatdya want from me?'

'Just thought I'd stop and see if you'd seen or heard anything that might be helpful.'

'Well I ain't, so you can just look somewheres else.'

'You'd be Will McAllister?' Levi asked.

'How'd you know that?'

'Marshal in Ten Sleep drew me a map,' Levi replied, still speaking slowly and pleasantly. 'You always meet strangers with a shot-gun?'

'You ask a lot of questions.'

'That's my job. You always meet strangers with a shot-gun?'

'Not as a rule, but there's been a lot of killin'.'

'Well, you met me with it. Now you better put it down before I wrap it around your neck!'

McAllister looked surprised and uncertain. He threw a quick glance over his shoulder and began to fidget. 'What you talkin' about? You ain't got nobody comin' behind me.'

Levi had eased his horse to within two steps of the homesteader. As he turned his head, Levi kicked his horse. The horse lunged forward. Levi kicked the barrel of the shot-gun aside. It fired harmlessly into the air. At the same instant, Levi slammed his pistol hard into the side of McAllister's head. He slumped silently to the ground.

'I'll let him think about that, and talk to him later,' Levi muttered to himself.

As he rode out of the yard, he scolded himself. 'That's twice in one day I coulda got myself killed. First I forget to check the corral, then I ride right up to a shot-gun. I can't afford any more mistakes like that.'

THREE

From his horse, Levi watched the scene unfold. The ranch was small but tidy, with a well-built house, a small livestock shed and a corral. When the man entered the yard, the door of the house flew open and two young children ran headlong toward him. He stepped from his horse and swept them both into his arms, hugging them and nuzzling their necks as they squirmed and giggled.

He sat them down as a rather plump, homely woman stepped out of the house. Less enthusiastic than their children, her joy in his homecoming was nonetheless evident. He watched them stand close, touching each other as they talked. Then the man moved toward the corral with his horse, his children bounding alongside. Levi was too far away to hear what they were saying, but the music of their voices carried deep within his soul.

He swallowed the lump in his throat, as he watched what he could never have. Any normal family life was outside any realm of possibility for him. He was almost inhumanly strong, incredibly quick and accurate with a gun, and able to whip any three men he had ever met. His pure physical prowess caused others to fear and hate him almost instantly. No woman would ever be willing to share the kind of life his unique abilities had thrust him into. Fate had dealt him a lonely hand. He accepted it, but the loneliness always rested like a dark cloud in the back of his mind.

He watched the young rancher walk across the yard to the small, tightly built house. Each of his children clung to one of his hands.

'Ain't right to bother 'em just now,' he mumbled, reluctant to let the atmosphere of a happy family depress him further. 'I'll talk to 'em later.'

In late afternoon he looked over the Banner ranch, nestled into a cleft of hills dropping down toward Meadowlark Creek. With timbered hills to three sides and an open slope downward to the east, it was a breathtakingly beautiful site.

'Smoky, that's as beautiful a spread as I've ever seen in a long while. I sure hope we get a warmer reception there than we've been getting. I'm starting to feel as unpopular as a preacher at a still.'

As he approached the house, a dog barked several times. A tall man with a great shock of grey hair stepped out on to the porch that ran around two sides of the house.

'Evening,' he called out. 'Get down and come in! You're just in time for supper.'

'Well, thanks,' Levi responded. 'I could stand a bait of grub if you're sure it wouldn't put you out any.'

'Not at all,' the rancher responded. 'You'd just as well put your horse in the barn and bring your bedroll in as you come. You will be spendin' the night won't you?'

The difference from the reception he'd been getting all day overwhelmed Levi with gratitude. The gratitude crowded that nagging warning back to the more remote corners of his mind. 'If you don't mind, I'd be happy to stay in the bunkhouse.'

'Won't hear of it. We got all kinds of room in the house. My name's Tom Banner. I'll tell my wife you'll be having supper with us.'

'Yeah, well, thanks a lot,' Levi responded. 'Oh, I'm Levi Hill....'

'The range detective out of Cheyenne?' Banner asked, suddenly more than just hospitable.

Levi tensed. The sense of being an outsider to the race of man returned with a rush. 'Uh huh. You heard of me?'

'I've heard of you. There ain't too many in this country that ain't. Your name's about as famous as Wild Bill Hickock around here. Everyone's a little excited that you was hired to solve things. Go put your horse up and come in.'

'I take it that killings must be pretty uncommon around here,' Levi probed.

Banner thought for a moment. 'Well, no, I can't say as bein' killed is anything too special. Happens, time to time.'

'I always figured that was something that could only happen to you once,' Levi observed dryly.

Banner looked confused for an instant, then broke into a chuckle. 'Well now, I guess maybe gettin' killed would be sort of a once-in-a-lifetime thing at that.'

'Supper's on the table, Tom.' A pleasant voice

spoke from the door into the kitchen.

Looking slightly embarrassed, Banner said, 'Well, now, here we are standin' here jawin' and me forgettin' my manners. Levi, this is my wife, Kate. Kate, this is Levi Hill. He's the range detective Hansen talked the sheriff into sendin' for.'

'How do you do, Mr Hill,' Kate responded. 'The whole country has been anxious for you to get here. If you'd like to put your bedroll in the guest room and wash up, supper is on the table.'

'Glad to meet you, ma'am,' Levi responded. 'Thank you, I'd be real happy to do that, just as quick as I get my horse put up.'

To himself, he thought, I've met a couple of folks today who weren't too thrilled with the idea of my getting here.

It took only a few minutes to take care of his horse and enter the house. 'Ann,' Mrs Banner called over her shoulder, 'would you show Mr Hill to the guest room, please, while I finish setting things on the table?'

Levi caught his breath as a young lady stepped out of the kitchen. She was no more than two or three inches over five feet tall. Raven hair cascaded in gentle curls across her shoulders. A hint of freckles bridged her nose. Her eyes jumped and danced with a life and vibrancy that was electric. Her eyes took in Levi, pausing for the briefest instant on the badge pinned to his shirt.

Kate said, 'Mr Hill, may I present Ann? Ann, this is Levi Hill. As soon as you're washed up, Mr Hill, we'll eat.'

Ann held out a hand to Levi. He took it almost

in a daze, not sure what he was supposed to do with it. She shook his hand with a firm steady grip that would have given credit to any man. She released his hand and turned toward the broad curving stairs that led to the upstairs bedrooms. 'This way, Mr Hill. I'll show you to your room, then show you where the washroom is.'

'Uh, please call me Levi, ma'am,' he said as the dam stemming his speech finally broke. He followed her up the stairs. 'When folks say "Mr Hill", I always look around for someone important.'

She flashed a quick smile over her shoulder at him as she answered. 'OK, I'll call you Levi if you promise never to call me "ma'am" again. I hate that word!'

'You've got a deal, ma'am. Uh, I mean, Ann,' he quickly corrected. He was rewarded by another of those flashing smiles. It dazzled him so completely he nearly missed a step.

He dropped his bedroll and rifle in the room to which she led him, then followed her back down to a small room just inside the side entrance. A marble-topped wash-stand held a basin and pitcher of water, with towels hanging above it. 'Just come on in the kitchen when you've washed,' Ann said as she gestured at the wash-stand. She disappeared through the kitchen door with another small smile.

Levi washed quickly, suddenly eager to join the others at the table. He wasn't sure whether it was to fish for another of those brilliant smiles, or to satisfy his hunger.

The table conversation dwelt on the murders for

a while, touched on the inevitable topic of weather, then moved on to happier topics. 'How many hands do you normally have on the place?' Levi asked conversationally.

'Nine, as a rule,' Banner responded. 'More at round-up, of course, but the permanent crew are all good hands who've been with me quite a while.'

Levi looked pointedly at Ann as he answered, 'If I know cowpokes, I bet you got a line all the time just waiting to work for you. I bet you would have, even if you didn't pay wages.'

Ann reddened slightly again and turned her attention to her supper. Platters of food were passed amid scraps of information and rangeland gossip. After supper they continued to visit for quite a while, then Levi excused himself and went up to his room. He considered quite a while before wedging a chair under the door knob. 'I guess it's foolish here,' he muttered to himself, 'but I just ain't easy sleeping inside four walls, without the door braced some.'

FOUR

It was still dark as Levi leaned against the top rail of the horse corral. He watched the first streak of light illuminate the eastern horizon. Much of the sky was overcast, looking a dull grey in the beginning light of the new day. Along the eastern horizon, there was a narrow band of clear sky. As he watched, the sun began to near the horizon, and a tinge of red began to spread. It changed the lifeless grey of the clouds into a soft magenta, then rose, then orange.

He had been fighting the turbulence of his thoughts since he had wakened, three hours before. The scene of the happy rancher and his family yesterday, had disturbed him deeply. All night he had tossed and turned as he dreamed of himself in that picture. He had done so before, but the face of the woman in the dream filled out. The woman was Ann, whom he had only just met that night.

He woke after his fitful sleep, feeling angry. He was a realistic man, and such dreams served only to make his loneliness more acute. He just didn't know how to control his dreams while he slept. He must find a way to do so.

He jumped as he sensed a presence near him. Whirling, his hand stabbed toward his gun. He stood that way, feeling foolish, as Ann smiled at him. She had walked up beside him and stood as he was, watching the sunrise. After that small smile she turned back to watch it without speaking. He did the same.

The drab grey of the overcast had looked smooth until the rising sun cast colours across it. Now it showed the uneven texture it really had. The deeper lines of cloud were greyish red, with the lower puffs increasingly red and brilliant. As they watched, the bottom tips of those caught fire, burning with a brilliance that rivalled the sun itself.

The canopy of colours tinged with fire spread from the eastern edge of the clouds until it reached more than halfway across the sky. It bathed the world and its two watchers in a ruddy glow of incredible beauty. They both watched wordlessly until the increasing light faded the colours into a drab, dull grey again.

'Nothing in the world more beautiful than a sunrise,' Levi observed softly.

'Except a sunset,' Ann responded softly.

Levi considered it a moment before he replied. 'Nope,' he asserted. 'Sunrise is the prettiest and best. Sunrise is the beginning, and it leads into the life of a new day. Sunset is just as pretty, sometimes, but it's the end, not the beginning, like death.'

'But death can be good and beautiful too,' Ann said. 'The end of things can be better than their beginning.'

'Maybe,' he said reluctantly, 'but only for someone that's old and sick and lived all the life they have a right to, and you know they're right with God, and all that.'

'That doesn't have to mean old,' Ann insisted.

'What do you mean?'

'Some people live all the life they have a right to, a long time before they get old. Sometimes the death of someone is the best thing for others, or for the land, or things that are supposed to happen.'

'I can't agree with that,' Levi argued. 'Death is always a waste.'

'Not always,' she insisted. 'If a coyote kills a rabbit, it's death for the rabbit, but life for the coyote. If the rabbit doesn't die the coyote will starve, or find something else to kill instead. Everything dies to provide life for something else.'

'Except people,' Levi corrected.

'Even people,' she kept arguing. 'Haven't you killed people?'

'Only when I had no choice. I ain't some hired gun who enjoys killing. I never kill if I can help it.'

'You always have a choice. You could let them kill you instead. Every time you killed someone, you decided their death would mean your life, and your life was better.'

Suddenly uncomfortable, Levi scowled. 'That isn't something there's a lot of time to think about when the chips fall.'

'No, of course not,' she soothed, 'but it's an assumption you make when you learn to shoot quick and straight. Whenever your life is threatened, you already know the right response.

It's to take somebody else's life to protect your own. You are saying, when you make that preparation, that someone else's death might mean your life, so his death will be good.'

Levi turned away from the corral. 'Well, I suppose you may be right, but there's the matter of law and justice, too. Anyway, this conversation sure got a long way away from a pretty sunrise.'

She laughed lightly. 'It did, didn't it? There ain't many people around I can discuss philosophical things with. I enjoy it.'

'Where'd you learn that kind of thing?' he asked.

'From Mrs ... from Mother. She was educated at a fine women's school in the East.'

'Is that so?' He marvelled. 'The folks who raised me, she was too. Some school in Pennsylvania. She taught us kids a lot of that stuff.'

Ann was intrigued at once. 'You mean she educated you?'

Levi nodded. 'Me and Myra. Myra was their girl. She was some younger than me. She was their own. They was just raising me, but she taught us both the same. That's why I still always carry along a couple of good books, and read from 'em when I have time.'

'Oh, you'll have to share them with me,' Ann said with enthusiasm. 'Did she teach you Latin and everything?'

Levi was suddenly a little defensive. 'Only some, and a little Greek, too.'

'Oh, that would be so fascinating!' Ann enthused. 'You must teach me some of those phrases. I think they sound so wonderful, and so full of the mystery of far away places.'

'I like the books better,' Levi said. 'They make those far away places real. When I read, I can forget who I am, and what I'm fated for, and live a story like I'm somebody else. It probably ain't too healthy, but I enjoy it.'

'I think it's perfectly healthy,' Ann responded. 'That's what books are for. If it wasn't for the escape that books offer, life would be too hard to tolerate.'

Levi agreed, but he was reluctant to say so. Instead, he said, 'Mrs Rudabaugh, that's the woman that took my ma's place, she always made us read some from the Bible every day, too.'

Ann's eyes clouded, and Levi could instantly sense her withdrawing from the conversation. 'I've never read it much,' she said. 'I think breakfast must be about ready. Maybe we should go in.'

They walked back to the house where breakfast was already being put on the table. Conversation held to general topics of concern to everyone on the range. He prepared to leave shortly after breakfast.

'If you need a place to hole up while you're scoutin' around, you're sure more than welcome anytime,' Banner told him. 'Fact is, if you're a mind to, you can just call that room you stayed in last night yours as long as you're around. Come and go as you feel the need.'

Levi shot a quick look at Ann. 'Well, thank you,' he said sincerely to Banner. 'I'll take you up on it, if you let me do a little work around the place from time to time.'

Banner grinned. 'You just catch that jaybird

that's shootin' up folks around the country. That'll be more'n enough to earn your keep.'

Levi rode out whistling an old ballad he hadn't heard in years.

FIVE

Levi's heart was soaring as he left the Banner Ranch, but his eyes were alert as ever. He constantly probed every ridge, every thicket, every clump of trees for any potential danger. Instead of feeling that he was riding into danger, though, he suddenly felt as if he were riding away from something that had almost destroyed him. He shrugged off the feeling with a scowl.

Topping a small rise he saw the abandoned buildings of the Binder homestead below him. There was a small house, an open shed for livestock shelter, and a small corral. A few trees had been planted in three rows along the west side of the house.

'Now there's a man who built for the future,' Levi explained to his horse. 'Planted himself a grove to shelter the house. Built the house small but solid, so he could add on to it as he needed. Set it where it would still be in a good place by the time he added a barn and a bunkhouse and a cook shack and whatever else he needed if he built it into a ranch. There was a man who had plans. All he needed was time and a woman, and he'd have made them all come true.'

For some reason he could not explain, his own words filled him with a sudden sense of imponderable sadness. He lifted the reins and the horse moved down off the knoll. He circled the house carefully, then got down from his horse. Leaving the reins hanging so the horse would stand where he was, he approached the front door. He pulled the latch string and the door opened smoothly and easily. His respect for the careful building of the man increased.

'Shame to see a man that careful get killed,' he muttered to himself. 'Men like that are the stayers that build a solid country.'

There was only one room. Matt Binder, being a bachelor, had no elaborate needs. The house was neat, orderly, and perfectly organized. A bed along one wall was still neatly made. The combination heating and cooking stove occupied the centre of the floor. Opposite the bed, a table with three chairs stood about two feet from the wall. A free-standing cupboard stood just beyond the table. Pegs in the walls provided places for hanging various items. The only thing out of place was a great deal of dried blood around the chair the hapless homesteader had been sitting in, when his throat was cut.

'That's odd,' Levi thought. 'It doesn't look like he even tried to move. He was either held, or he was so surprised he couldn't figure out what happened till he was too near dead to move.'

The remains of a meal were in a pan and a skillet still sitting on the cold stove. Two plates and silverware sat on the slide-out counter top of the cupboard. A cake, well nibbled by insects, sat beside the plates. 'Even built his house mouse-tight,' Levi mused. 'All that time and there still ain't been any mice in here eating the grub.'

He was still turning the details of the place over in his mind when he returned to Ten Sleep. He stabled his horse at the livery barn, carried his bedroll and rifle to his hotel room, then dropped in at the marshal's office.

'Evenin' Marshal,' he greeted as he walked in.

The town marshal looked him up and down. One hand swiped at the abundant growth of his handlebar moustache. It sagged down both sides of his mouth, giving him a perpetually dour expression. 'Evenin' Hill,' he responded. 'Got our case all solved yet?'

Levi smiled dryly. 'Yup. I guess you could say I have,' he responded, watching the marshal's eyebrows shoot up. 'I figure someone is downright mad at a bunch of folks. He kills 'em. Only thing left to figure out is who and why.'

The marshal's eyes flashed fire for just an instant, then switched to a twinkle. 'Well, now, that's great!' he rejoined. 'You got all the hard stuff figured out. I'm sure glad we called in a famous expert to take care of that.'

'Who was Binder courtin'?' Levi asked abruptly.

'Courtin'?' The marshal's expression went immediately serious. 'Nobody that I know of. Why?'

'Just wondered. Looks like he was expecting someone special the day he got killed.'

'Why's that?'

'Well, he had a pretty good meal whipped up. Dishes for two laid out. Baked a cake. Ain't too many bachelors that could bake a cake, or would, unless they was expecting someone special.'

The marshal chewed the corners of his moustache while he thought about it. 'Makes sense, sure 'nough,' he said finally. 'Don't know why I didn't think of that. Still and yet, I don't know who it could've been. Maybe it was someone else's girl, and then someone else found out.'

'Could be, or maybe somebody else's wife,' Levi agreed. 'Too early to guess yet.'

Levi rose from his chair and left the marshal's office. He ate supper at one of the two cafés Ten Sleep boasted, then walked over to the Big Horn Saloon.

He paused just inside the heavy front door that stood open, sizing up the interior. It was a typical Wyoming saloon. A potbelly stove stood in the centre, with a bar the length of one wall. Tables stood randomly around the floor. A stairway led to a hall, lined with rooms where the inevitable girls plied their ancient trade. A piano nobody was playing stood at the rear wall. He walked up to the bar, close to the far end, away from the door.

'You must be the investigator from Cheyenne, by the description,' the bartender greeted him. 'What'll it be?'

'Got coffee?'

'Sure. Most generally give it away to the guys that already bought too much of the other stuff though.'

He brought a steaming mug of thick black coffee, and Levi laid a nickel on the bar. The bartender shoved it back at him. 'I'll get you twice next time,' he said. 'You don't drink at all, or just not today?'

'Be a long dry spell if I didn't drink at all,' Levi grinned.

'That's a fact.' The bartender grinned back.

He moved back down the bar to another cowboy who was holding up an empty glass. Levi sipped his coffee, studying the patrons of the bar through the thin wisps of steam.

A thin, dark man slid sideways off a chair by a rear table. He looked almost serpentine as he slunk toward the door. Levi noticed the hard glares of several of the bar's patrons follow the man to the door and beyond. As the bartender worked back close to him Levi nodded toward the front door. 'Who's the half-breed?'

'Alfred Spotted-Pony,' the bartender responded sourly.

'Folks don't seem too kindly disposed toward him,' Levi observed.

'That's the truth,' the bartender replied curtly. 'It ain't just that he's half Indian, neither. He don't never work, don't wash, don't change clothes, and don't live nowheres. He's just around, and he's always got whatever money he needs. The girls charge him double, whenever he wants one, but he always just pays it and don't complain. Someday someone's going to find out where he gets his money, and we'll have ourselves a hangin', like as not.'

'You seem pretty sure wherever he gets it is crooked.'

'Where could he get it that ain't?'

'Bein' an Indian don't make him a thief,' Levi insisted.

A stir from a table near the door interrupted the

conversation. Three men rose together and walked toward him. That familiar sense of danger welled up instantly. 'Who are these fellows?' he asked the bartender quickly.

'Art's the blacksmith, in the middle,' was the answer. 'The other two work for Banner's Box-A.'

Levi's glance instantly absorbed the details of the biggest man. He stood nearly six feet tall, with shoulders that threatened to bulge through the oversize shirt. His exposed forearms looked like tree limbs that tapered to huge hands with forge-blackened fingers. Raw power emanated in ripples as he moved.

'So you're the great Levi Hill!' the one identified as the blacksmith said, as the three approached. 'We was sorta wonderin' why you thought you could ride in here and take care of our problems like we was a bunch of school kids.'

Levi moved his mug of coffee carefully away. 'Maybe the sheriff figured I'd better,' he responded cheerfully, 'so you school kids would have a chance to grow up.'

The blacksmith's face reddened. His companions instantly backed up a step to allow him room. Before they or the blacksmith knew what happened, Levi's fist shot out. Carrying the weight of his body and the full strength of both his arms and his legs, it exploded visciously on the tip of the blacksmith's chin.

The fist landed with the sound of an axe striking wood. Levi felt the shock of it travel clear through his arm and shoulder, down into his ribs. The blacksmith never even saw it coming. His eyes went out of focus. He sat down, falling backward with his arms flopping outward and lay motionless in the sawdust.

In the instant of stunned silence that followed, Levi took a quick step backward. His gun swept up smoothly, covering both of the others. 'Now suppose one of you fellows tell me what this was all about,' he commanded.

The two looked stupidly back and forth between Levi and their fallen companion for fully half a minute. Nobody in the bar moved. No sound broke the breathless silence.

Levi spoke again. 'You,' he designated one of the men with his gun barrel. 'What's your name?'

The man swallowed twice, then finally answered, 'Dusty Brickner. Me'n Art and Dutch don't like you hangin' around and shinin' up to Ann like you been doin', that's all. We seen you an' her a-talkin' and gigglin' out by the corral. We don't want her gettin' messed up with no hired gunman. My Gawd you hit him hard!'

'There's no sense in hitting a man gently,' Levi said smoothly. 'Now you boys listen, 'cause I'll only tell you this once: I have a job to do; I'll do it whether you want me to or not, whether you like it or not; if you get in my way, you'll get hurt.'

He holstered his gun, turned his back on the gaping pair, and walked out. When he was clear of the place, he let out a long sigh of relief. He spoke to himself. 'I hope I don't have to fight that man again. He'll be lookin' for that Sunday punch next time.'

SIX

The first red streaks of sunrise coloured the tips of the Big Horn Mountains to the east. Levi followed the Norwood River north out of Ten Sleep. About mid-morning he sat a small rise of ground looking down on another homestead.

He rode slowly into the yard, hand nearly touching his gun butt, every sense keen and alert. He caught a hint of movement in the corral, so he stayed where he could see both house and corral without turning. 'Hello the house,' he called out.

'I heard ya,' a nasal voice called back from the rickety corral. 'You must be Hill, that investigator fella. I seen that badge you're a-wearin'. I heard you was snoopin' around.'

Levi kept his horse situated so he could see the man while still keeping the house in his field of vision. 'You Bud Malvern?'

'How'd ya know that?' the nasal whine bristled.

'Marshal told me the lay of the land around, who lived where,' Levi answered, trying to sound nonchalant.

'Well, he didn't need to tell you nothin' 'bout me. I got no ties to anythin'. I'm just scratchin' out a livin', and not hardly that. This here's a hard country, you know.'

'You have any idea what's behind the killings?'

Malvern glanced at Levi quickly, then just as quickly averted his eyes. As they talked his eyes occasionally flitted across Levi's face, but he never allowed their eyes to meet fully.

'No more idee than anyone else,' he whined. 'Reckon someone knows them better'n most, and figures they ain't fit to live. Might even be right, ya never know.'

'You saying they deserved to die? Why?'

'I didn't say they deserved it,' Malvern quickly backtracked. 'I just said maybe somebody thought so. Anyway, they's a couple of 'em likely did, anyway.'

'Like which ones?' Levi pressed.

'Now don't you go badgerin' me,' the home-steader's whine rose a decibel. 'I'm just a hardscrabble homesteader, tryin' to keep from starvin' clear to death. Just 'cause they was a drop or two o' bad blood 'twixt me'n Binder and maybe McClatchey, that don't mean nothin'.'

'Bad blood?'

The homesteader spat a streak of brown tobacco juice in the general direction of the corral, then swiped the back of his hand across his mouth. He wiped the hand on the leg of his trousers.

'Jest say I warn't sorry to see them two get it, and let it go at that,' he whined. 'But that don't mean I had nothin' to do with it!'

Levi's voice turned flat and hard. 'Maybe you'd better tell me what brought the bad blood between you.'

The homesteader looked everywhere but at Levi

for several moments of heavy silence. He kept shifting his feet like he wanted to be anywhere but here. Finally he said, 'Ain't nothin' that'd help you none. Me'n Binder, we got in a little fight once. Sneakin' coyote busted me in the mouth afore I was even set, then whupped up on me good.'

'What was the fight about?'

'It was just one o' them things. We was drinkin' some. I said somethin' he didn't like. I coulda maybe whupped 'im if'n it was a fair fight.'

'What about McClatchey?'

'He just thought he was some high an' mighty rancher. He always kept makin' remarks about where I maybe come from and where some o' his calves was maybe goin'. He didn't never accuse me o' nothin', but he kept a-pickin' away all the time.' The whine picked up speed. 'Pickin' and pickin' like a bunch of magpies on a fresh brand! There warn't never no call fer him to keep pickin' on me like he done. I ain't got nothin' in this world but just this here hardscrabble homestead and me not hardly eatin' reg'lar, and him all the time pickin' and pickin'. You can't blame a man fer gettin' tired o' that. I didn't kill 'im, though. I didn't kill neither one of 'em. But I ain't shed no tears, nor blowed no snot fer 'em neither.'

His litany of self-pity recited, the air seemed to go out of him. Levi fought to keep his lips from curling in disgust. 'Well, I'll take your word for that, for now. I may want to talk with you again, though.'

The homesteader looked at him for the barest instant. Fire flickered behind the façade of blandness, but his eyes were quickly averted again.

Levi rode from the yard at an angle where he could keep the man in the corner of his eye until he was into the edge of a narrow neck of timber. As soon as he was in the trees, he abruptly changed course, quickening his pace to outdistance any possibility of ambush.

'That man gives me the creeps, Smoky,' he said at last.

Levi entered the Banner ranch yard in the afternoon. He was already out of the saddle before anyone spotted him. Tom Banner was walking from the barn to the house and stopped abruptly. 'Well, Levi!' he said with obvious surprise. 'I sure didn't see you ride in. You're just in time for supper. You'll be staying the night?'

Levi relished the feeling of almost childlike eagerness that surged in him. 'I'd be obliged. You know what they say about feeding a stray dog.'

Banner chuckled. 'Well, if strays were as welcome as you, they'd all be fed. You go ahead and put your horse up and come on in. I'll tell Ann to set another place.'

He let himself in by the side door and washed up before walking on into the dining-room. Banner greeted him as he stepped in the door. 'Just as well grab a chair, Levi. Ma and Ann are just settin' the food on.'

Levi's spirits lifted magically. He sat down to the smell of fresh hot bread, roast beef, and hot potatoes. They ate quickly and in comparative silence, but he kept stealing furtive glances at Ann as he ate. Every time he did, a lump caught in his throat.

When they had finished, they each sat back with a cup of coffee to let their supper settle around the quiet and easy conversation. Levi suddenly felt more at home than he could remember feeling in many years. He found himself craving Ann's bright and bubbly comments, her flashing smile or her quick giggle. He kept having to remind himself Tom and Kate Banner were even present.

The conversation turned inevitably to the subject of his investigations. 'Do you have any good ideas yet?' Banner asked.

Levi pulled himself from the deep pools of Anne's eyes with an effort and turned to the rancher. 'Not really,' he admitted. 'I have a feeling they're connected. Do you know any common thread tying all the murdered men together?'

'What do you mean?' Kate asked.

'I can't find out anything they all had in common,' Levi explained. 'If there's something all of them had in common, that could indicate the motive, and maybe who did it.'

They mulled over the string of murders, much as Levi and Marshal Hansen had done, with as little result. They found nothing that would tie them all together.

Finally Levi spoke. 'Well, it seems like the only thread I can see so far is that they were all fine men, with no enemies, and no reason for anyone to want them dead.'

He was startled by the sudden fire in the depths of Ann's eyes. She spoke heatedly. 'The fact that nobody knows anything bad about some man doesn't mean there's nothing bad there. Some men in this country have done unspeakable things in the past, and nobody even knows it.'

Levi pursed his lips thoughtfully. 'That's just the point,' he said. 'If I ask enough questions, sooner or later I'll run across somebody that knows what that is.'

'And if you don't?' Banner asked.

'Then I'll have to figure out a different way to track down the killer,' Levi responded. 'Tell me, how long had the men who were killed been in this country?'

The Banners looked at each other thoughtfully. 'Well, I hadn't thought about that,' Tom said. 'There aren't any newcomers involved, I guess. Caulder was the newest, and he came into this country about twelve or thirteen years ago, riding with a prospector. Caulder stayed around and started riding for one ranch or another. I guess the others were all here ahead of him.'

'Well, there's something,' Levi said thoughtfully. 'At least they were all in the country a long time. That's not especially good, though. That means I'll have to ask questions about a lot of years, not just lately.'

'You mean you think it might have been something a long time ago that ties them together?' Kate asked.

'If there even is a common thread,' Ann said. 'Isn't it possible that there is more than one killer, and more than one reason?'

Levi smiled at her. 'What are you trying to do, girl? See how confused you can get a poor old range detective?'

Her eyes suddenly lost the troubled look, twinkling and dancing in response. 'Of course. I like to see big strong men admit they don't have all the answers!'

Kate rose from her chair. 'This conversation is going to get us all in trouble,' she announced. 'Ann, please help me clear the table. We'll get the dishes done up while the men go in the other room and solve the country's problems.'

Banner rose, chuckling. 'Levi, I believe we have been dismissed. Shall we go sit in the front room?'

When they were comfortably seated, Levi said, 'That daughter of yours is quite a girl.'

Banner chuckled. 'She sure is quite a girl all right. She isn't really our daughter though. Well, I guess she is, but she wasn't always. Me and the missus never could have any kids. When I brung her home it was like a breath of fresh air to Kate.'

'You brought her home?' Levi said, confused.

Banner looked troubled. 'Yeah. Well, you see, her folks got themselves killed, and her only about nine or ten. I brung her home, and she fitted in like she'd always been here. From that first day, she just flat refused to talk about her life before. She sure has been a joy to us.'

The similarity with his own tragic childhood struck Levi like a sudden blow, but he refrained from mentioning the fact. Instead, he asked, 'Her name isn't Banner, then?'

'Nope. She mostly uses Banner, and that's sure fine with us, but legal-like I guess her name's still Spencer.'

The dreams came again, that night. He and Ann lived scenes of pastoral beauty and domestic bliss. Tonight, though, he didn't wake every time. He just smiled in his sleep and snuggled into the softness of the bed.

SEVEN

'Well, good morning,' Levi greeted. 'You sure do get up early.'

'So do you,' Ann replied brightly. 'Where are you planning to ride today?'

The morning had dawned clear and sharp. The first rays of the sun, along with Ann, had caught up with Levi as he saddled his horse. Ann was dressed for riding.

'Why?'

'I just haven't been off the ranch for quite a while. If you didn't mind, I thought I might ride with you.'

Levi's heart leaped, then plunged with the realization he couldn't possibly involve her in his work. 'I'd sure enjoy that,' he said slowly, and with honest regret, 'but I'm not sure it'd be good. It might get dangerous.'

She flashed one of those smiles and he felt his resolve melt. 'I really won't be in your way, and I'm not afraid of someone taking a shot at you.' Her chin tilted tauntingly. 'Besides, I might just spot something you'd miss.'

'Well, well. One week you've been listening to me and already you're a better detective than I am, huh?'

She giggled. 'You'll never know unless you let me come along.'

'Do your folks let you go riding around the country?'

A hint of a cloud passed across her eyes, but was gone in an instant. 'They do now,' she said slowly. 'They didn't for a long time, but I've pretty much ridden where I wanted the past year. I really do know the country. You could use a guide.'

He hesitated, knowing his heart was getting the better of his head. Why, after learning to be content with loneliness, was this girl's company so pleasant and so important? Sighing he said, 'Well, I guess it'd be all right today. You want me to saddle your horse?'

Her eyes flashed fire for just an instant, then twinkled at him. 'My horse is already saddled, cowboy. I'm not a greenhorn.'

Neither of the Banners offered any objection. They rode out together, following Meadowlark Creek south and east.

They climbed steadily for a while. The creek sang a loud and constant song as it tumbled across rocks and gravel. Then the land levelled again, broadening into a wide flat valley verdant with grass and timber. Elk paused in their grazing to watch them, undisturbed. They spotted several deer and an occasional black bear, rabbits, grey mountain squirrels, and a couple of porcupines.

As they topped a small rise they spotted a pair of coyotes almost 300 yards ahead of them. Levi drew the rifle from his saddle scabbard, and was surprised that Ann already had her own rifle in her hand. Acting as though they were controlled by the same mind, they both turned their horses sideways to the coyotes, which started to trot toward their left.

'I'll take the left one,' Ann said.

'OK,' Levi responded, bringing his rifle to bear on the other one. 'You shoot first.'

He had no sooner said it than Ann's rifle barked, followed at once by the retort of Levi's rifle. The lead coyote dropped instantly, while the trailing one, which Levi had shot, spun in a circle two or three revolutions before falling and lying still.

'Nice shot,' Levi praised. 'You handle that rifle almost as good as a man.'

Ann's face turned crimson and her eyes flashed before his grin relaxed her and she returned the grin. 'Why thank you, mister famous lawman,' she said with an exaggerated drawl. 'You just flatter little ol' me too much! I must say, though, you seem to need a little larger target than I do. I shot mine in the head.'

Levi's eyes whipped back to the two coyotes lying motionless, then back to Ann. 'You shot him in the head? From three hundred yards?'

She affected a look of wide-eyed innocence, continuing the heavy drawl. 'Why, of course. The only way a girl like me can outshoot you is to shoot mine in the head.'

Levi looked at her for a moment, then lifted his reins. 'This I've got to see,' he said, nudging his horse into motion toward the dead coyotes.

He stepped down and looked closely at the one

she had shot. There was a neat hole just below the left ear. Much of the other side of the head was blown away. His own coyote was shot just behind the front leg, exactly where he had aimed. Wordlessly he remounted and they continued the way they had come.

They had ridden nearly fifteen minutes before he found the right words to ask the question that was echoing in his mind. 'Why did you shoot him in the head?' he asked finally. 'Aside from trying to outshoot me, that is.'

Ann did not smile. 'We have to shoot them,' she said, 'but they don't really deserve to die. I mean, they have to die, because they kill so many calves and lambs and baby deer and everything, but they only do that to live. They're just being coyotes. They don't deserve to suffer. The one you shot didn't live very long, but long enough to hurt. He was spinning so fast to try to get away from the pain.'

'So you'd rather take a chance on missing?'

'I didn't take a chance on missing. I don't miss.'

He restrained his retort; instead, he asked, 'Where'd you learn to shoot like that?'

'I've known how to shoot ever since I can remember. I could outshoot both my parents by the time I was six, and they could both shoot awfully well.'

'Your mother could shoot, too?'

Ann bristled just a little at the surprise in his tone. 'Of course. Most women in this country can shoot.'

'That's true,' he admitted at once, 'but most of them don't shoot really well. Most of them just get by when they need to, and don't really like to.'

There were several minutes of tense silence between them. He was as puzzled by her defensiveness of her remarkable ability as he was of that ability itself. Finally he asked, 'Do the hands on the Box-A know you can shoot like that?'

She giggled, suddenly totally feminine again. 'No. Those poor boys would be mortified if they knew I could shoot circles around them!'

Impulsively he asked, 'What happened to your folks?'

Her eyes instantly turned the flat colour of hardened steel. Her mouth tightened to a straight thin line that made her rich, full lips all but disappear. 'I don't talk about that,' she said shortly.

Levi was instantly sorry he had asked. A grey cloak draped across his soul when her smile vanished. Desperately he cast about in his mind to find something to say that would change the subject, but he could think of nothing.

They were still riding in silence when they emerged from the timber above the Hazelton homestead. They sat in the edge of the trees studying the building site for several minutes. Levi almost forgot Ann beside him as his habit of caution came into play. He noted all the places a person might be expected to be. He mapped out the least dangerous approach, and best route of escape if he encountered hostility. He tried to get an idea of the occupant's character from the buildings he had erected.

The homestead itself was a rough copy of most of the homesteads in the area. The house was small but snug against the weather. The barn was just an open-sided cowshed for shelter from the wind. The open side faced a large corral, made of pine poles. The yard was neat, void of the usual junk and garbage pile somewhere behind the house. 'Wonder what he does with his trash?' Levi wondered aloud.

'They dump it in that little ravine on the other side of the house,' Ann offered.

'Tidy sort, isn't he?'

'They,' Ann corrected. 'This place belongs to Clint Hazelton. He is a neat and tidy sort. So are his wife and two kids.'

That squared with the toys lying in the yard, and Levi nodded. 'You mind staying here and covering me? I'll mosey down and see what they know.'

'Why?' Ann asked. 'Why not just ride in and visit?'

'Habit, I suppose,' Levi responded. 'Anyway, I've walked into trouble I didn't expect too many times the past few days.'

Ann nodded wordlessly and swung down from the saddle. She drew her rifle from its scabbard and took up a position beside a tree, where she had an unbroken view of the yard below. Feeling more confident than anytime he could remember recently, Levi rode boldly down into the yard.

'Hello the house,' he called out from the edge of the yard.

A young woman, wiping her hands in her apron, stepped out the front door of the house. A small child clung to her skirt. Another peered around the door frame. 'Good morning,' she responded. 'Won't you get down? My husband just went over to the crick for a bucket of water. He'll be back in just a few minutes.'

Levi swung down from the saddle, feeling more like a visiting neighbour than an investigating lawman. 'Thank you,' he answered. 'Don't mind if I do. I'd be obliged for a drink of water, too, if you have one handy.'

The woman nodded. 'There's coffee on the stove, if you'd rather. Oh, good morning, Ann! I didn't see you.'

Levi started and turned, just in time to see Ann step down from her horse. 'Hello Sarah,' she greeted the homesteader's wife. 'Levi wanted me to watch from the trees to make sure everything was OK here before I came on down. When I saw you and the kids I knew it was. Hello Nicholas. Hello Jeremiah.'

The two boys grinned at her, but made no move to reply. Just then a man stepped around the corner carrying a bucket of water in each hand. 'Well, we have company,' he greeted, stopping. 'Hello Annie.'

'Hello Clint,' Ann responded at once. 'Clint, Sarah, this is Levi Hill. He's the range detective.'

Clint grunted, then nodded his head toward the house. 'Just as well come on in and sit a while,' he said.

They made their hands comfortable around steaming mugs of coffee. Levi found himself fighting the sadness any scene of home and happy families always raised in him. To distract himself from its oppression, he broached the subject of his investigation rather abruptly. 'Have you folks heard or seen anything that might shed some light on the killings?'

He noticed at once the covert look Sarah shot at her husband, and waited for the reply. 'Not a thing, really,' Clint responded slowly and almost too cautiously. 'We haven't been in the country all that long. 'Bout five years, I guess, but we know most of the folks around. I don't think anybody but the killer knows who's doing it.'

The silence hung heavily for several moments. Levi knew he had something more than that on his mind, but he was reluctant to badger obvious friends of Ann. He raised his eyebrows enquiringly, first at Clint, then at Sarah. Sarah finally spoke, addressing her husband. 'But you do have an idea, don't you Clint?'

Clint shrugged uncomfortably. 'Well, an idea, yeah, but that's all it is. More gossip than anything.'

'Why don't you tell me anyway,' Levi suggested. 'Sometimes gossip has some sort of basis in fact.'

Clint shrugged again. 'Well, mind you it's just a wild idea. You met Bud Malvern? He's got a homestead along Meadowlark Crick. Real whiner, to talk to.'

Levi snorted in spite of himself. 'I met him. From down south somewhere, ain't he?'

Clint nodded. 'So he says, anyway. He acts like a first-class coward. Gossip has it, when he gets mad he's hell on wheels.'

'That so?' Levi encouraged.

Clint nodded. 'Just sorta seems funny for a fella to act so whiny, when he don't have to be. He ain't somebody I'd ever turn my back on.'

The conversation moved on to other things, but

Levi kept musing on the idea that Malvern was not who he pretended to be. He'd have to do some checking on that.

EIGHT

After their visit with the Hazeltons, Levi and Ann rode out, returning the way they had come. Neither spoke for a long time.

Levi finally broke the thoughtful silence. 'This is the last homestead up this way, isn't it?'

Ann nodded. 'The Johnson ranch is up higher. It's about three miles on up, at the head of Meadowlark Creek. Do you want to ride on up there and talk with them?'

Levi thought about it for a while. 'No, I guess not, today. Let's ride back toward your place, and I'll go on into town tomorrow.'

They stopped for lunch in a grove of trees with a clear spring bubbling out from the rocks. Its waters tumbled in a soft musical cascade toward Meadowlark Creek below. Ann produced some smoked beef slices from her saddle-bag. Levi built a handful of fire to make coffee. He added some biscuits from his provisions, and felt he was eating a royal banquet, just because of Ann's presence.

They talked of everything and nothing. The trill of her laughter was interspersed with penetrating questions and sage observations that surprised him with their depth. She alternately elicited responses from his mind and sparked reactions from his heart. They talked and revelled in each other's company until half the afternoon had passed.

Reluctantly, at last, Levi rose to leave. 'We've wasted most of the day,' he lamented. 'We'd best get back.'

'I didn't realize it was so late,' Ann responded. 'I don't know when I've enjoyed talking with anyone so much.'

She stood close in front of him. Her head was tilted back to gaze up into his face. The westering sun sent peaks of light through wispy strands of her raven hair. Her eyes shone as she gazed into his. The blue of his own eyes deepened as they absorbed the darkness of hers. They looked into each other's eyes wordlessly for several breathless moments. Then, almost as though he were unaware of his actions, he bent his head toward her. The fullness of her lips filled the whole of his awareness, waiting slightly apart.

He couldn't remember really kissing a girl since he was a kid, but it seemed totally natural. She responded to his kiss willingly, and they were in each other's arms.

He kissed her lightly and awkwardly at first. Then he grew bolder, showering her lips, her face, her nose, her eyes, the sides of her neck with his kisses. She responded eagerly, stroking the hair along the back of his head and neck, repeatedly searching for his lips with her own. The tide of desire kept rising within Levi. He felt himself losing control. He released her and stepped back.

'We, we better back off a little,' he said breathlessly. 'We're about to do something we better not.'

Her arms still held on to his, and she continued to look into his eyes. 'Oh, Levi, I've wanted you to notice me so much. I felt like some brazen hussy asking if I could ride with you today, but I just wanted to be with you, and I knew you wouldn't ask me. You're so different from the cowboys and homesteaders. You make me think, and I've told you things I've never told anyone before. Oh, Levi, please don't leave here when you're finished.'

Levi swallowed hard several times before he could trust himself to answer. He turned from her, looking off across the folds of mountain. Finally he turned back to her. 'I guess any talk about that'll have to wait until I do what I came here to do. Right now I sure feel like I don't ever want to go anywhere you aren't.'

She came into his arms again. He kissed her, long and tenderly, then pushed her a little distance from him. 'We'd better get started back toward the ranch. It'll be dark before we get there if we're not careful.'

Her eyes danced at him. 'Afraid to be out after dark with me?'

He grinned back at her, feeling suddenly more totally relaxed than he had ever felt in the presence of a woman. 'Yup. I ain't responsible for my behaviour when I'm with a pretty girl alone after dark.'

'Oooh, sounds exciting,' she giggled at him.

They packed the things from their meal and caught their horses, mounted and rode out. From time to time, when their horses moved close enough, he would reach out a hand and touch her, as though to reassure himself she was really there and all this was really happening to him. It was all so impossible. He had lived for years with the knowledge that such things could never be a part of his life, his world. Then, so suddenly, it had happened to him. He wanted to laugh, to sing, to yell at the mountain tops.

As they approached the ranch, he spoke of the subject uppermost in his mind. 'Uh, Ann, would it be real presumptuous if I was to ask your folks if I can court you?'

The light peal of her laughter sparked tingles clear through him. 'And just what do you think you were already doing up there in the trees?'

'Uh, well, I mean, serious like. I mean, I don't mean I wasn't serious up there or nothin', but, but, well, I don't want to feel like we're sneakin' around like a coupla school kids,' he blurted.

She laughed again. 'I would like very much for you to ask permission to pursue me, Mister Hill. But be warned, I may have serious plans for you.'

Impulsively he leaned across to her and kissed her lightly. She kept a hand on the side of his face and looked into his eyes for a moment. 'I think I love you,' she said softly, 'and I don't even know you.'

He kissed her again, then sighed a heavy sigh of happiness. Sure comes on a guy sudden, he thought as he turned his horse toward the yard, with her close alongside.

They put their horses away, rubbed them down and gave them a double handful of oats. They stole another quick kiss in the barn, then went into the house. Kate looked at them both as they entered. 'Well, you two look absolutely radiant,' she observed.

Ann's face coloured and Levi coughed a little. He went on into the front room, leaving Ann to help Kate with the supper.

When the meal was finished and there was a lull in the conversation, Levi cleared his throat. 'Uh, Tom, Mrs Banner, there's something I'd – we'd like to say, er ask. I mean, well, uh, I'd like permission to court Ann.'

Tom Banner's eyebrows shot upward, but Kate's expression didn't change. 'I saw the way you two glowed when you came in,' she said.

'So that's the way the wind blows,' Banner said. 'Awful sudden, ain't it?'

Levi nodded with a concerned expression. 'I know it is, and I know we don't really know each other all that well. I can't explain why we both feel like we do, since we've only known each other a few days. But, well, I guess maybe that's what courtin' is supposed to do, ain't it? Give us a chance to get to know each other better.'

'Well now. I guess I don't have all that much to say about it,' Tom responded. 'Ann isn't a little girl no more. But she is still our girl. I can't say I'm real happy to have a range detective with a reputation bigger'n Wyoming, come courtin' her. Especially one that's going to be leaving as soon as his job's done here. Where would that leave Ann?'

Levi paused thoughtfully for a while before he answered. 'I guess I can't answer that till the time comes,' he said, 'but I already told Ann I wouldn't leave this country without her unless she runs me off. I can't be a range detective all my life. Sooner or later I'll be looking to have a place of my own. If, if things was to work out between us, I guess Ann is the reason I'd like to do that.'

Banner considered it for several heartbeats, then looked at his wife. She smiled back at him with a look that indicated the matter was settled regardless of what he said. He sighed. 'Well, I guess every cowboy on the place is going to have his heart busted when they figure out how the wind's blowin', but that's gotta happen sooner or later. I just hope every hand I got don't quit at once.'

Ann stood up and began to clear the table, but Kate stopped her. 'I'll do the dishes tonight. Why don't you and Levi go for a walk or something.'

Levi almost leaped from his chair and looked enquiringly at her. She smiled at him. 'Mr Hill, would you do me the honour of escorting me on a tour of the premises?'

He bowed sweepingly. 'Miss Banner, I would be most honoured to make you acquainted with your ranch yard, and "the soft moon's glow that caresses it",' he quoted.

'Oh, my, you're poetic as well!' she teased.

Laughing like children they headed for the door. As they stepped off the porch he felt her hand slip into his. As her fingers intertwined with his, he felt a thrill pass through his whole being. His steps bounced with a joy. So this is what bein' in love feels like! he exulted silently.

The moon was fully up when they went back into the house and to their own rooms. He didn't know anyone was still up until he heard Kate tell Ann goodnight through the wall of their bedrooms.

He chuckled to himself. Can't blame them for being a little protective. I bet Banner was watching us every minute. What a girl! How could I ever get so lucky? How could I feel like this, when I've only known her a week?

He fell asleep remembering the sweetness of her lips against his, the feel of her body pressing against him. His job, and that nagging sense of imminent danger, were not in his mind, or in his dreams.

They should have been.

NINE

The way a day begins carries no hint of its dangers – or its pleasures. The first streaks of dawn were illuminating the eastern horizon when Levi caught up his horse and saddled him. By the time he went in to breakfast his things were tied behind the saddle and he was ready for the road. Ann met him at the kitchen door.

'Good morning, handsome lawman,' she purred. 'Do you mean to ride off and leave me here all alone?'

Levi took off his hat and held it to hide their faces from Kate, who was busily preparing breakfast. Behind its shelter, he kissed Ann swiftly and ducked away. 'I have to go into town and ask about some things, then have another talk with our friend, Malvern,' he explained. 'I'll probably be gone three or four days.'

Ann's eyes clouded at the words. 'Three or four days?'

Levi grinned broadly. 'But you gotta promise you won't get lonesome and trade me in for one of your dad's cowpokes while I'm gone.'

She smiled back at him. 'If you stay gone too long, I just might.'

With an exaggerated toss of her head she

marched off to help Kate carry the platters of food to the table for breakfast. Still smiling within himself, Levi joined them for their usual hearty breakfast. He was still marvelling at the bubbling joy in his heart as he rode out.

He crossed Ten Sleep Creek and skirted widely around the town of Ten Sleep. Swinging north ahead of the river's bend, he headed for the homestead of Bud Malvern. He was riding up a long slope about a half a mile short of his destination when he felt a light tug at his shirt sleeve. An instant later the report of a rifle reached his ears. He dove from his horse, rolling as he landed. He lunged to his feet, looking wildly about for any kind of shelter. It felt like minutes before he spotted a small outcropping of rock. He dived behind it.

He heard a second report of the rifle as he left his horse. A third shot showered rock fragments from beside his head as he dove for cover.

Realizing the rocks were too small to conceal him, Levi lunged from behind them. Running in a zigzag pattern, he headed toward a large clump of brush twenty yards to his right. He heard the malevolent hiss of a bullet whipping past his ear as he ran. A fifth shot tore leaves and twigs from the brush into which he made a headlong dive.

He rolled several feet from where he landed, then lay still. His chest heaved. He tried to still the hammering of his heart. When he had gulped several gasps of air he felt for his gun. It was still in place.

'Well, at least I didn't lose my six-shooter,' he panted.

He squirmed on his stomach to a position that allowed him to see through the brush, scanning the direction from which the sounds of the shots had come. There was nothing in sight.

His horse stood about a dozen steps from where he had left him. His head was up and his ears forward, looking toward the same spot Levi kept studying.

Seeing nothing, Levi squirmed backward on his stomach, until he had retreated deep enough into the brush to be concealed. Then he raised to a crouch and began to assess his situation.

The brush he occupied was comprised of willow and buckbrush, with a few wild rose bushes along one side. It had formed where a small trickle from a tiny spring oozed out of the hillside, following a shallow channel down the hill. The brush covered only about half an acre, then gave way to tall grass that fringed the trickle as it wound its way down to a deeper depression 400 yards away.

Levi scratched his head. 'Now that fella's got me pinned down pretty good. He's clear outa pistol range, and he's got a rifle. It sounds like maybe a forty-four-forty. If I can stay outa sight long enough, I might be able to get down to that draw, then circle around him.'

He went back into the brush and squirmed on his stomach to where he could see to the top of the hill again. As he peered through the brush, a bullet tore the ground a few inches from his head, showering his face and eyes with dirt. He squirmed frantically backward. He rubbed at his eyes until he could see again, swearing under his breath.

'Now how could he see me in that brush from that far away?' he asked himself softly. 'I wonder if he's got some kind of a glass or something.'

Moving to the other side of the brush, he squirmed into the lowest part of the shallow channel. Keeping his head down, he ignored the icy wetness of the spring's trickle. He squirmed steadily backward down the hill. He attracted no fire.

When he reached the bottom of the hill he raised his head furtively to determine which direction held the best cover. He crawled head first along the bottom of the shallow canyon. When he had crawled nearly 500 yards he entered another brushy area. There he finally dared to raise to a crouch to better assess the terrain.

The brush he had now entered maintained a thick growth as far ahead as he could see, circling slowly downhill toward his left.

'Must be that draw that opens into the crick just above Malvern's homestead,' he muttered to himself. 'Oughta be able to circle the sneakin' coyote from here.'

Keeping low in the brush, he ran crouched from cover to cover until he had circled completely around. When he thought he should be within sight of the point of attack, he stopped behind a cluster of rocks until his breathing returned to normal. Then he cautiously inched his head above the rocks to scan the ridge. It commanded a view of the hill he had been riding up when shot at.

At once he spotted his attacker. Bud Malvern lay in a similar cluster of rocks, completely hidden from the bare hillside below him. He had a niche in the rocks through which he could see the entire field of fire, without himself being visible at all. His rifle lay at his right hand. He held a telescope with which he was carefully examining the brush in which Levi had taken cover.

Rising from his place of concealment, Levi slid the thong from the hammer of his pistol and eased it into his hand. He walked softly and carefully until he was less than fifty feet from the hidden homesteader, then he spoke.

'Don't even move, Malvern.'

The homesteader exploded with impossible speed from his prone position. He whirled, leaping upright as he grabbed his rifle. He dove in a long roll coming to his feet nearly twenty feet from his original position, levelling his rifle from the hip even as he reached his feet.

The rifle in his hands barked death a split second too late. Levi's bullet had already slammed into his chest, spoiling his aim. The bullet passed harmlessly over Levi's head, but he levered another shell into the chamber, firing again just an instant after Levi's second slug shattered his shoulder. He tried desperately to lever a third round into the chamber as the third shot from Levi's .45 smashed into him. He continued his efforts until he had the rifle cocked again. Levi had to shoot him a fourth time before he succumbed to the death so rapidly overwhelming him.

The homesteader glared at Levi as he vainly tried to lift the rifle, then finally dropped it and slumped to his knees. His snivelling, whining manner was gone. His lip curled in derisive hatred as he tried to speak.

'Shoulda killed you that first day. Knew you'd figure me out. You still lose, though. I didn't kill, kill....'

He coughed once. Blood spewed from his mouth. He fell forward on to his face and lay still.

Levi stood silently, keeping his gun on the dead man. Finally he heaved a great sigh. He shelled out the spent cartridges from the cylinder of his revolver, replacing them with fresh ones from his cartridge belt. Then he replaced the gun in its holster, slipped the thong on to the hammer to keep it in place, and walked over to the dead homesteader.

Using the toe of his boot, he rolled the man over on to his back. His eyes stared, blank and sightless, at the sky. Two flies, already drawn by the smell of blood, lit unheeded on his face and began their silent feast. Kneeling beside him, Levi went through his pockets. Finding nothing, he left the body and walked to the house. He carefully searched for anything that might shed light on the man's action. He finally found, lying on a cupboard shelf, a letter addressed to 'Arthur Kelley, General Delivery, Dodge City, Kansas.'

Levi carefully opened the worn and wrinkled letter. 'Musta kept this around a long while,' he mused.

He read, *Art. I done told Masterson the names of all us boys what tried to rob the train to save my own skin. The others is all caught, but if you get this letter quick enough maybe you can get away somewheres and change yore name. Dave Rudabaugh.*

The last name was the same as the family that

had raised Levi. He had never heard of any of their relatives named Dave. If there was an outlaw in their family, they had never mentioned the fact. He frowned at the irony, then read the letter again.

'So that's what he was hiding from,' Levi mused. 'Must have gotten scared and thought I figured out who he was. A guilty conscience is a relentless enemy.'

He pocketed the letter and returned to where his horse still waited. The horse was munching grass, trying to eat around the bridle bit. He looked reproachfully at Levi.

'Boy, that sure beats all, old Smoky,' Levi scolded. 'Here I am fighting for my life, and you're getting sore 'cause I didn't take the bit out of your mouth first, so you could eat. Some friend you are!'

Mounting, he rode back past the dead homesteader without looking at him, to the corral. He caught the dead man's horse, saddled him, found an old tarpaulin and a lariat, then returned to the body. He shooed away the flies that were already swarming on the corpse, then rolled it in the tarpaulin, tying it tightly around the body with the lariat. Snubbing the homesteader's skitterish horse close to the saddle horn of his own mount, he hoisted the man's body across the saddle and lashed him into place. Then he stepped into the saddle, released the lead rope of the homesteader's horse enough to give him room to follow comfortably, and started toward Ten Sleep.

By the time he reached the marshal's office in Ten Sleep he had a small crowd following along. Hansen was standing in the door waiting for him when he arrived.

'Another victim, or the killer?' Hansen asked without preamble.

'Neither.' Levi replied just as abruptly. 'Bud Malvern. Tried to drygulch me. His real name's Art Kelley. He's wanted in Kansas for an old train robbery. I guess he figured I was on to him.'

'Think he killed the others?'

'Nope. A man who's hiding from his past don't usually attract lawmen with a rash of killings. Besides, he said he wasn't, when he knew he was dying. A man doesn't lie then.'

Levi handed the marshal the worn letter. He read it, then folded it carefully. He chewed the corners of his moustache thoughtfully for a minute, then nodded. 'I 'spect you're right. Well, I'll take him over to the undertaker, then we'll talk some.'

Levi spent the next hour or better rehashing everything he knew with the marshal. He was impressed with the local lawman. 'You're a good lawman for a small town.'

Hansen chuckled. 'Yeah, folks seem to think anyone with any brains has to go live in a big city somewhere. Fact is, I decided anyone with brains would leave the city.'

'You've lived back East?'

Hansen chuckled again. 'Raised in Virginia. Educated in Boston. Came West as an accountant for the railroad. I like it out here. A man doesn't have to stand on his degrees. I'm fully aware there is no "i" in "crick", no "r" in "warsh" and "pertneart" is not a real word, but in this country it matters not at all. Here a man can stand on his own manhood and his own ability, and do just about any decent thing he's man enough to do.'

They walked together to one of the cafés and ate supper, continuing their visit. Then Levi went to his room at the hotel. He thoroughly cleaned his pistol, slid it back into its holster, propped a chair under the doorknob, and climbed wearily into bed. In spite of his weariness, he stared sleeplessly at the dark ceiling for a long while.

TEN

Levi paced his hotel room like a caged lion for nearly an hour. He lay on the bed for a few moments, trying to doze, then lurched back to pacing the floor. Finally he grabbed his hat and his rifle and headed out the door.

He stopped at the marshal's office. 'Arlo, I'm riding over toward the Marchant ranch and talk with them, then up over the hogback to Banners. I'm just as sure as I can be that Malvern ain't our man.'

'Suit yourself,' the marshal replied, 'but if the murders stop we're going to almost be forced to accept that he was the perpetrator you know.'

'I know that. It's possible he was. We'll just have to wait and see. Meanwhile I'm gonna keep nosing around and see what else I can scare up.'

'Well, try not to scare up any more shady pasts. You've given the undertaker enough business for a while.'

Smiling ruefully, Levi left. He got his horse from the livery barn, saddled up, tied his bedroll and supplies behind the cantle, and rode out.

He couldn't stay in a black mood too long. The shadow that had hung so bleakly over his mind was gone. The spectre of being a man who must live out the whole of his days in loneliness had weighed on him more than he had ever realized. He remembered now how many times, and how painfully, he had turned from every scene of a happy family and home, because it was something he could never have.

Now he smiled as he thought of Ann. It was still such a wild, impossible dream. When Sarah Ferguson had agreed to be his girlfriend in school, it had felt like this. Then he had been backed into a corner by Butch Hadley and his two friends. Levi had whipped the three of them, all bigger than himself, and beaten them severely. He hadn't understood, then, Sarah's reaction. Instead of hailing him as her mighty hero she turned away from him in disgust. It was the end of the only romance he had ever experienced. Until Ann.

Ann already knew he was a fighter. She already knew he made his living with his gun. She already knew he had killed other men, and they talked openly about it. It didn't matter to her! She loved him anyway! He had no doubt their courtship would end in marriage and a home. Home! The word sang in his mind with the joy of a thousand impossible dreams.

He crossed the mouth of Meadowlark Creek and continued onward, reaching the Marchant ranch by early afternoon. Margaret Marchant stepped to the inevitable front porch as he rode into the yard. He rode directly to the house and took off his hat.

'Afternoon, ma'am. You'd be Mrs Marchant?'

'Yes, I'm Margaret Marchant.'

'My name's Levi Hill.'

'I've heard of you,' the rancher's wife said. 'Ann seems to think you're pretty special.'

Levi felt his face redden. 'Well, I guess that goes both ways,' he acknowledged. 'She just may force a footloose man to put down some roots.'

Mrs Marchant laughed brightly. 'Get down and come in, won't you? Have you had dinner?'

'Well, thank you,' Levi said, stepping down. He wondered if she would have dared ask him into her house if not for Ann. Just knowing another woman loves a man, seems to make that man different, trustable.

'No,' he replied. 'As a matter of fact I guess I didn't realize it was past dinner time yet, Mrs Marchant.'

'Please call me Meg,' she replied as Levi stepped on to the porch. 'Ike is out with the hands, but you're welcome to stay until they get back. Come on in and sit down. I'll fix you some cold meat and cheese.'

He entered the quiet coolness of the spotless kitchen and sat down at the table, placing his hat on the floor beside him. He felt like a stranger in some new world, where people regarded him as a part of their own race.

Meg kept up a bright conversation as she sliced bread and laid it out for him with slices of cold roast and cottage cheese. He ate more than propriety dictated without realizing it. As he did so, he filled her in on the events of the past day.

'Do you think Bud was the killer, then?' Meg asked.

'I honestly don't know,' he replied.

'It has been so terribly upsetting to all of us,

having this go on,' Meg confessed. 'We thought the country was finally becoming civilized. There are two churches in town now, and a regular court when the circuit judge comes, and it isn't the wild west any more. Then something like this starts happening and it turns the clock back fifty years. My boys are almost old enough to marry now, and I don't want them raising families in a wild country like I did.'

'There's always trouble and violence,' Levi argued, 'even back East.'

'I know that,' she admitted, 'but it's not the usual thing. When it happens back there, it's a real oddity. The law is there to deal with it, and things are nearly always peaceful. We can't say we've improved on what the Indians had in this land until we can have that here too.'

'I guess it's coming,' Levi observed. 'Even here they bring in a lawman, now.'

Meg was thoughtful for a long moment before she spoke. Then she said, 'That's true. We haven't really had a case of people trying to take the law into their own hands since Ann's parents.'

Levi's attention snapped alert at the words. 'Ann's parents? What happened to them?'

'Hasn't Ann told you about them?' Meg asked.

'No. She just said she didn't talk about that, and it upset her that I asked, so I haven't pushed it.'

Meg sighed heavily. 'That has been her defence since the day it happened. She has always refused to talk about it at all. If it is mentioned, it gains nothing except to quell that bubbly personality of hers, so we all learned to just not talk about it. It was pretty awful.'

'What happened?'

There was a long and heavy silence before Meg answered. 'I suppose you have a right to know, if you're really serious about Ann. Her folks had a homestead along the Norwood south of Ten Sleep, but her father wasn't much good. He was lazy, and something of a gunman. He never really worked his homestead, and never took care of his cattle, but he always had plenty of money. Everybody else kept losing cattle, and it got pretty obvious after a while that Ollie was stealing them.'

'Was there any proof?'

'I honestly don't know. I know it reached the point where there wasn't any question about it any more.'

'What happened?'

'Well, a bunch of ranchers and their hands rode over to confront him with the evidence. They were all sitting their horses in front of the house, as I understand the story. Ollie had two guns in holsters and a rifle in his hands. Then Marie, Ann's mother, is supposed to have started shooting from inside the house. Four men were down before they could even get their guns out, but the rest of them started shooting back. Both of Ann's parents were killed. They found her hiding in the house after it was all over.'

'They shot her mother too?'

Meg nodded. 'They claimed they didn't know who was shooting from inside. It didn't make any difference since she was shooting men out of the saddle. Anyway, Tom Banner took Ann home and raised her. He sent hands over there to keep things up, and prove up on the homestead in her name, but I don't think she's ever been back there.'

'How old was she?'

'Ten or eleven, I think.'

'And she never talks about it?'

'No. I guess maybe she just blocked it out of her mind, because she couldn't deal with it.'

They visited for the better part of an hour, but Levi had a difficult time concentrating on anything Meg was saying. His mind kept returning to Ann and the hurt she must have felt, must still feel, must still carry in some hidden recess of her being. He longed to reach out to her, tell her he knew, but he would have to keep that knowledge to himself until she elected to tell him about it.

Finally he rose to leave, thanking Meg for the lunch and information. Then he rode quickly from the yard. He angled directly up across the ridge separating the valley that housed the Marchant ranch from Banner's Box-A.

He was scrambling up over a rimrock in late afternoon when he thought he heard the sound of a shot carried faintly on the breeze. He pulled Smoky to an abrupt halt and raised in the stirrups to listen, but no further sounds broke the silence. Thoughtfully he continued on his way.

Across the top of the hogback he descended a long, gently sloping hill resplendent with wildflowers. He was skirting a large clump of aspens huddled around a small spring when he heard a shout. Turning in his saddle he saw a lone rider waving to him from a thousand yards away along the slope. He waved back and stopped.

As he watched, the other rider spurred to a run toward him. As the distance narrowed he recognized Ann. He kicked Smoky into a run to meet her. They met in a flurry of dust and leaped from their saddles to cling to each other as though they had been separated for an eternity.

When the fervour of their joy had cooled, Levi stepped back and looked into the flushed radiance of her face. Her eyes burned with a brightness that looked almost eerie. She clung to him as though he might run away.

'Oh, Levi, it's hot out here in the sun. Let's go over there in the shade,' she said as she pointed to the aspen grove by the spring.

He agreed eagerly. They held hands as they led their horses to the edge of the trees. They tied them there, then walked on alone into the quiet and welcome shade. At the spring they paused to drink from the sharp coldness of the water, then stared at each other for a long moment. Then Ann, her eyes glistening, reached her arms to him. He pulled her hungrily to himself.

His eagerness was more than matched by her own. He was both delighted and a little bit frightened by the fervour of her ardour. It was as though something had torn away all her restraints. She held him breathlessly, avidly, frantically, as though her need for him was a desperate thing.

The sun was scarcely an hour above the Absaroka Mountains in the west when Ann smoothed her hair and prepared to leave. Her mood was much more subdued, but her eyes still shone with such a dancing brightness it made a lump in Levi's throat as he stared into them. It was Ann who finally spoke.

'It's going to be way past dark by the time I get home. The folks will be worried. Maybe you shouldn't ride in with me this late. It might not look too good.'

The idea was new to Levi, and he considered it. 'Might be just as well if I didn't. I wouldn't want any of the hands to start saying a bunch of stuff. I'll just go ahead and camp here by the spring, and ride on in tomorrow. Will you be all right, riding alone at night?'

She made a face at him. 'Of course I will! I love you, my darling.'

They clung to each other hungrily for a moment, then she pulled away and returned to her horse, mounted and rode away. Once she turned in the saddle and waved to him. Only then did he turn to his own horse. He hobbled his front feet, removed the saddle and bridle, and set up camp in a sheltered nook near the spring.

The dark loneliness of those shuttered chambers of his mind were gone. He could never remember feeling so good.

Something in his mind whispered, Too good to last. He thrust the thought away, and revelled in thoughts of love.

ELEVEN

He didn't want to sleep. He wanted only to savour the memory of the feel and smell and taste of the woman he loved more than he had ever known a man could love.

He did sleep, though, nearly an hour later than usual. He woke with a start, noting the sun was already well up in the sky. He rolled from his blankets muttering under his breath, feeling guilty for sleeping so late. He fixed a hurried breakfast over a small fire, caught his horse and saddled up. He decided to ride back over the hogback then follow up Meadowlark Creek to the Kaiser ranch before returning to the Box-A.

He was barely started when circling buzzards in the sky caught his attention. He stopped and watched them. 'They got something dead, Smoky,' he informed his horse. 'They're landing and new ones coming in, so they're feeding. Guess we best check it out.'

He urged the horse to an easy lope. He rode lengthwise to the long slope that led down from the ridge he had crossed the afternoon before. It was several minutes before he realized he was going in the same direction from which Ann had ridden to meet him. 'Sure hope it ain't trouble up there, fella,' he again addressed the horse. 'If it is, it couldn't have been too far from Ann yesterday.'

After a while he slowed the horse to a trot, not willing to tire him too quickly in the day. It took two hours for him to reach the birds of prey.

As he rode out of a small stand of spruce, his stomach lurched. About fifty yards from the trees, in a small depression that might have once been a buffalo wallow, a man's body lay stretched in the sun. Buzzards sat on and around the body, tearing at all exposed pieces of flesh, in rapt indulgence at their macabre feast. Levi spurred his horse to a run, shouting and firing his gun into the cluster of buzzards, killing several. The birds reluctantly lifted into the air, but hovered close. Some lit on the ground at what they deemed a safe distance, awaiting his departure to renew their grisly meal.

Levi dismounted beside the dead man. He took a deep breath, then looked full into his face. There was no recognizable face to see. The wart-necked birds had eaten more than half of it away. It was impossible to even guess what the man had looked like.

He turned away. 'Let's see if we can find his horse, and see where the shot came from,' he said out loud. 'He's got a hole in him big enough for a buffalo gun, but I can't tell if it started out that way or the birds been eatin' there too.'

As he started to ride out in search of the dead man's horse, the birds moved in on their meal again. He stopped, shot another buzzard and watched the rest back out of range. He sat there, pondering the situation for several moments. Finally, with a heavy sigh, he dismounted and untied his bedroll from behind his saddle.

He took a blanket and rolled the dead man in it, lashing it securely around him with his lariat. Then he remounted his horse. 'Sure hate to ruin a good blanket, old boy,' he continued his habit of speaking to his horse, 'but I can't let 'em keep eatin' on him. Let's find that horse.'

An hour later his circling search found the man's horse. It had wandered to a trickle of water, and was munching grass as best it could with the bridle bit still in its mouth. With the reins dragging, it was an easy matter for Levi to catch it, and he returned to the dead man. The buzzards were still crowded around the corpse, but were frustrated in their efforts to get at the coveted meal.

Levi dropped the horse's reins, knowing he would wander slowly if at all, and studied the lay of the land. From the position the body had been in, and the direction the bullet had entered, he guessed at an outcropping of rocks near the hill's crest as the place from which the shot had come. He goaded his horse up the hill to investigate.

The ground behind the rocks was clean of all traces. 'Not a track,' he muttered. 'Clean as a whistle. Too clean. No tracks of animals, or birds, or anything around those rocks. Looks like the right spot, but the drygulcher did a real careful job of blotting out tracks.'

Dismounting, he walked in tightening circles around the cluster of rocks, searching for any sign that might have been missed. He was ready to give up when his eye caught an irregularity in the ground beside a clump of scrub greasewood. Scarcely visible to any but the keenest eye, he could make out part of the outline of a booted foot.

Levi's blood surged as he realized he had just found his first solid clue. An expert tracker, he knew he had only to find one clear track and he would be able to recognize it again, wherever he saw it. It might not be evidence that would convict in court, but it would tell him with total certainty who had waited in these rocks and struck with deadly efficiency. He searched the entire area again, watching until his eyes began to feel gravelly with the effort, but there was not a complete track to be found. All he had to go on was that one partial track.

'Small foot,' he mumbled. 'Awful small. Can't be too many men runnin' around that small. Might even be smaller'n that half-breed's foot, but it sure ain't him. He wore moccasins, and wouldn't likely change to boots when he was sneakin' up on someone.'

He thought he could make out a slight irregularity along the outside of the sole of the boot that made the track, but he couldn't be sure. There was no other trace of the assailant's presence. He finally did find the branch of greasewood used to wipe away the tracks. 'Headed east,' he said to nobody in particular. 'Either that or carried his broom east to make me think so if I found it.' He thought about that for a while, then shook his head. 'Nah, not likely. Musta headed east.'

Returning to the corpse, he loaded it on to the

horse in spite of the animal's vigorous, wall-eyed protests. He had to tie one hind foot to the saddle horn, holding it off the ground, to keep him still enough. When he released the horse's leg it was all he could do to keep him under control until he became accustomed to the gruesome burden.

Leading the horse and its residue of humanity, he followed Meadowlark Creek. He passed within a mile of the Banner place. He looked longingly in that direction several times, but duty bore him past, and on toward Ten Sleep and the marshal's office.

TWELVE

'Another good man's dead. We're no closer to a solution than the day the great and famous Levi Hill rode into town.'

Levi's ears reddened, but he said nothing. Arlo Hansen was in a foul mood. He had been sure Bud Malvern was the killer who had been terrorizing the area over the past several months. He had the motive, the means, the disposition, everything. Now, with Malvern dead, another murder had been committed.

The marshal had identified the man from his horse and personal effects. 'Gerhardt Kaiser,' he growled. 'Everyone called him Gert. I'll have to tell Sven Olsen, from the Mercantile Store. Him and his wife are friends of Gert and Mabel. They'll have to go out and break the news to Mabel.'

He stood there chewing the corners of his moustache, then spoke to Levi again. 'Go get yourself something to eat, if you still got any appetite. Then come back to the office. We'll start over.'

Levi corrected him. 'Not quite. We have a lead. I'll tell you about it then.'

He took his horse to the livery barn and turned

him over to the hostler, then walked to the closest café and ate dinner. When he returned to the marshal's office, Hansen was still chewing furiously on his moustache.

'I just figured out why you never eat,' Levi grunted. 'You get all the nourishment you need from that moustache you keep chewing.'

Hansen glared at him. 'Dang right,' he agreed sourly. 'Especially if I've had soup lately. It holds enough to keep me going for a week. All I have to do is keep sucking on the corners.'

'Guess I'll have to grow me one,' Levi said with mock seriousness as he seated himself across the desk from the marshal. 'Pickin's get a little slim once in a while. Be nice to have something along to tide me over.'

The marshal agreed with matching seriousness. ''Course you got to watch it some when you're on a long trail. Tends to get a little sandy sometimes.'

'I'll keep that in mind,' Levi said, finally grinning. He sobered again at once. 'I found the first solid thing I've found to go on at all, today. It ain't much. Found part of a track. Only one, and it wasn't very clear. Who do you know with a fairly small foot? Like I say, it ain't very clear, but I'd guess he doesn't weigh over a hundred and forty, maybe less.'

The marshal leaned back, eyes suddenly bright with interest. 'Well, now. That does narrow things down a bit. Let's see…. The bronc stomper on the Box-A is a little guy. Dusty Brickner.'

Levi nodded silently and waited.

'There's a homesteader up by Paint Rock Crick, Nate Edgar, who's about the same size. There's a couple small riders on the McClatchey ranch. Don't know their names, but I've seen 'em a few times in town. There's a couple trappers up the crick toward Buffalo ... was the track a boot or a moccasin?'

'Ridin' boot.'

'Well, that leaves out the trappers. Guess that leaves out Spotted-Pony too. Aw, I guess they's a dozen fellows around that would fit the description. Can't think of any right off-hand that would have a reason to do all the killing, though.'

'Malvern's size would fit, too,' Levi mused, 'but I guess we know it wasn't him.'

They mulled the matter between them for the better part of an hour, then Levi changed the subject.

'Arlo, I got another thing I'd sure like to ask you about. I guess you probably know by now, I'm kinda sweet on Ann Banner.'

'Heard as much,' the marshal admitted. 'Seen upwards of a dozen cowboys drowning their sorrows over at the Big Horn when they decided maybe she'd settled on you. I can sure 'nuf see her shinin' up to you, you bein' a romantic hero come into town to make it all safe for everyone. I gotta admit, though, I'm sorta surprised that you'd be so taken with her so quick. You plannin' to stay around this country, or you just havin' fun?'

Levi reddened at the implied insult, but he bit back his response. Instead he said, 'I don't know if I'll stay around this part of the country or not. Haven't thought that far ahead, yet. I been a lawman a long while. I never had anything much to do with women.'

'Just like all the other starry-eyed cowboys, even if you are a lawman,' the marshal groused. 'She's pretty settled. She shore ain't likely to be agreeable to runnin' around the country with a lawman.'

'You're probably right. We'll just have to talk that out. I guess maybe I could homestead around here, and run against you for town marshal or something.'

The marshal ignored the bait, and continued, 'She owns a proved-up homestead up the Norwood, you know.'

Levi grew more sombre. 'That's part of what I wanted to ask you about. Ann just won't talk about her folks at all. I wondered if you could maybe fill me in on that whole story. You were marshal here when they got killed?'

The marshal shook his head. 'No, but I was deputy sheriff, working out of Worland. It was two, three years after that I took the town marshal's job here in Ten Sleep. I guess I know as much about it as anyone. Bad deal.'

'Was her dad a rustler?'

The marshal looked at him closely before he answered. 'There wasn't any doubt. He sold some hides that had the brand worked over. You could see it plain as day on the back side. There was always calves showin' up with his brand, still sucking a cow that belonged to someone else. One of Kaiser's hands saw him selling a dozen head of cows clear down at Casper that had Banner's brand. He had a bill of sale with Banner's name on it, but Banner said he didn't sign any.'

'Then why didn't you arrest him?'

'I was wanting to, but the sheriff wanted evidence that was a little tighter before we moved. About half the evidence we had was second-hand stories and such. Anyway, the honest ranchers just got tired of waiting, and decided to run him out of the country.'

'That's when they went to their place?'

The marshal nodded. 'Rode out there with a good twenty men. They were pretty cool-headed though. It wasn't a lynch mob, or anything. There were several level-headed ranchers heading it up, and the rest were their hands. They thought it'd be better to just get rid of the problem than drag it out any longer.'

'Do you know what was said?'

Again the marshal nodded. 'I could just about repeat the conversation word for word. I questioned at least a dozen of the ones who were there, and they all told the same story. It seems that Wink Johnson did most of the talking. He told Spencer they had evidence he was stealing cows from just about everybody, and the sheriff was about ready to arrest him. Instead of seeing him get hanged and his family be without a husband and father, they'd sooner see him ride out of the country and not come back.'

'What did he say?'

'Well, he got pretty defensive and denied everything. Then he got mad, and told them to get off his place or he'd start shooting. Just when things were really tense, a horse fly bit Scruffy Jenkins, one of Kaiser's hands. He swore and swatted it. Spencer heard him swear and saw him move quick. He must have thought he was going for a gun. He dropped his rifle and had both his pistols out before anyone could even move. He shot Scruffy. From inside the house someone opened up at the same time. There were four men on the ground before anyone could unlimber a gun. Then every gun in the outfit opened up on either Spencer or the window the other shots were coming from. When the shooting stopped, Spencer and his wife were both shot to pieces. Six men in the other bunch were dead, and all but half a dozen were wounded in one way or another. One of them died later from gangrene.'

They both sat in deep silence for a long while. It was Levi who finally broke the silence. 'And Ann saw it all.'

The marshal watched him closely, then answered slowly. 'I guess nobody knows what she saw, or why she wasn't hit with all those bullets flying around like hornets from a busted nest. When they went into the house she was sitting beside her ma, just brushing her hair with her hand. She didn't cry. She didn't scream. She just kept brushing her ma's hair and saying something to her over and over that nobody could hear. I guess they all just stood there and watched her for several minutes, because nobody knew what to do. Finally Banner went over and took her hands and got her to stand up, and talked to her.'

'Do you know what he said?'

'Everybody heard him, and everybody remembered just exactly what he said. He said, "Child, I'm so sorry. We didn't want anyone to get killed. We wanted your daddy to leave with you and your mother, so nobody would get killed. Now I don't know what to do. I do know that my wife and I have always wanted a little girl. If you will come home with me we'll take care of you, and try to find whatever family you got. If we don't find 'em, well, I guess I'd just be plumb honoured if you'd be our girl".'

'And she did?'

'Without a word,' the marshal affirmed. 'They said she looked at her ma once more. Then she took ahold of Banner's hand and walked out with him, and never looked back. As far as I know she has never mentioned it since. She's never gone back to the place. Banner saw to it that the place was proved up on, and that the title was put in her name, but nobody's ever seen her near it.'

There was another long and heavy silence. Again it was Levi who finally broke it. 'Do you remember who all was in the posse?'

'Well, now, it wasn't a posse,' the marshal corrected. 'There wasn't a lawman with them, and it wasn't authorized. It was just a bunch of men, but yes, I guess I could remember who all was there. Let's see, there was Banner and Kaiser and Johnson and Marchant and McClatchey. They were the ranchers. The rest were their hands. There was Shorty Murdock, Moody Zelmer, Wade Renfro, Oscar Gunnison, Matt Binder, Ralph Whitmer, Sonny Laue, Win Caulder, Bill Murphy, Scruffy Jenkins, Will Nelson, Bob White, Art Littleton, Josh Miller, and, let's see, the hand with the game leg from McClatchey's spread, ... aw, now what was his name? Anyway, he was one killed. Oh, and Zack Pardee, he's the one that died of gangrene. Oh, and Sven Olsen, the guy that runs the Mercantile Store now. He was ridin' for Johnson then, before he married Joe Boswell's daughter and inherited himself a store. I might have missed a couple, but that's just about all of them.'

There was another long silence. This time the marshal interrupted it. 'Why'd you want to know all their names?'

Levi shrugged. 'I don't know, really. It was such a terrible thing for Ann to have to go through, I guess I just want to know as much as I can about it. Sure looks like she'd talk about it.'

The marshal nodded. 'That's always bothered me, if you want to know the truth. Everything I know says you got to talk about stuff like that to get over it. Seems like she just blocked it out of her mind, forgot it ever existed, and started over. It sure hasn't seemed to bother her. She's about the bubbliest little old girl I've ever known, just as long as you don't try to talk about her folks.'

Levi agreed wholeheartedly. 'She sure can turn the sunshine on, just by that smile of hers,' he said. 'I guess I never knew what it was to be really happy till she said she loved me. I'll tell you, Arlo, she is something! I just can't believe a ramblin' range detective could ever get that lucky!'

The marshal chuckled at the unaccustomed disclosure of feelings. 'You sure do have a case on her, all right, don't you?'

Levi grinned self-consciously. 'I sure can't deny that. I always wondered why a tough cowboy turned into a blushing stammering idiot when the right woman came along. I guess I found out.'

The marshal chuckled again, then rose from his

chair. 'Well, I guess the next thing is to try to find somebody to match that track, huh?'

Levi also rose. 'I guess I'll nose around town for a while, then tomorrow or so I'll mosey back out toward Banner's. If we don't uncover something by then, I'll just start circling around the country asking more questions.'

THIRTEEN

Levi was sitting at a table against the back wall of the Big Horn Saloon. He spotted the marshal as soon as he walked in. When his eyes met Levi's he started toward him at once, returning greetings from the bar's patrons as he came.

He sat down and spoke quickly and seriously. 'Swing back over to the office. Stumbled on to something, maybe.'

Levi's eyebrows shot up questioningly, but the marshal ignored the look and rose from the table. He moved around the bar, sizing up the mood and the people present with the practised ease of a true professional, then went back out the front door. Levi waited two minutes, then followed.

When he reached the marshal's office, Hansen was already seated at his desk waiting for him. He had a sheet of paper in front of him, with a list of names. Several of the names had check marks in front of them. 'Look at that!' he said, as Levi sat down.

Levi scanned the list. 'That's the list of men in the bunch that killed Ann's folks.'

The marshal nodded, his eyes shining. 'Now tot off the ones that are checked. Every man who's been killed, aside from the one you killed, is on that list!'

Levi felt like the world had retreated to some distant unconnected place, leaving him suspended in the middle of a formless void. His own voice seemed to echo into that void as he breathed, 'Somebody's killing everybody in the bunch that killed Ann's family!'

The marshal nodded grimly. 'The ones that're scratched off are the ones that were killed there. Laue, Jenkins, Nelson, White, Littleton, and Pardee. Jack Miller was killed a couple years later when a horse stacked him up. Busted his neck. Moody Zelmer lit out of the country. Ain't heard anything of him since. Oscar Gunnison got caught out and froze to death in a blizzard about four or five years ago. That only leaves six men out of that whole bunch who are still alive.'

Levi followed down the list, naming the surviving members of the ill-fated band of vigilantes. 'That leaves Johnson, Banner, Ike Marchant, Shorty Murdock, Ralph Whitmer, and Sven Olsen.'

'There's more,' the marshal said. 'I don't know what good it's going to do but I think I can name the killer.'

'You can?'

He nodded. 'It took a long time for me to dig through my memory to identify the bells that were ringing, but it finally clicked. Along about that time, the sheriff's office got a flyer mailed up out of New Mexico, looking for an outlaw named Clay Allison. A note with it said they understood his sister was married to a man named Spencer, and lived somewhere around this area. The description of Allison was a slight man, about five-feet-six.'

'Did he ever show up around here?'

'Nope. Only other time I heard of him, there was a story going around about him getting mad at a dentist in Cheyenne. Don't remember what the deal was, but Allison started pulling the dentist's teeth with his own pliers. Rumour says he's a killer, likes to kill from ambush, and would kill a man for snoring as quick as Hardin did.'

'So you think he found out what happened, learned who was involved, and is slippin' around out there in the mountains, killing everyone involved in his sister's death?'

The marshal thought about it for quite a while. 'Could be,' he said without conviction, 'but not too likely. A loner camped around this long would attract attention. Some cowpoke or sheep herder or trapper would stumble across him, or people would see where he'd camped, that sort of thing. No, it's much more likely he's somebody we know, using a different name, working for one of the ranchers, so he can come and go without arousing suspicion. Bunkhouse gossip would eventually give him the names of everyone involved, and whenever he has a chance he kills one of them.'

Levi rolled it over and over in his mind, looking for a flaw in the marshal's logic. He could find none. 'That's pretty good,' he admitted finally. 'Maybe you ought to go to work for Pinkerton.'

'Someone's gotta do the job,' the marshal shot back. 'You been here all this time and ain't got it done.'

Levi grinned. 'Well, thanks to the marshal of Ten Sleep, we're getting closer. That should narrow it down to a man thirty-five years old or older, who came into this country somewhere around a year ago.'

'That's right, on all but the age,' the marshal corrected. 'He was only sixteen when the law was looking for him from New Mexico, so he wouldn't be thirty yet.'

'Have you checked on his whereabouts since then?'

'Nope. Had no occasion to, until now. I did send a wire to the Colfax County Sheriff's Office in New Mexico, though, asking for current information. I should have an answer back in a day or two.'

'Dusty Brickner!' Levi said explosively.

'What?'

'Dusty Brickner! The hand who works for Banner. He's been there just over a year. He fits the description like a glove fits a hand. If he's Ann's uncle, it makes sense he'd get a job on the place where Ann is. And he seems to be real protective of her. Him and two of his friends tried to scare me off when I first came, supposedly because they thought I was paying too much attention to her.'

The marshal mulled it thoughtfully. 'I heard about that little episode. According to the story, you knocked him out, flung him over your shoulder with one hand, and carried him home!'

Levi grinned a little sheepishly. 'It was Dusty who seemed to set that deal up. It sure fits.'

The marshal carefully agreed. 'It does seem to add up. I don't know a thing about him. He never makes himself stand out at all. That could be to keep from attracting attention. He's got a person- ality a lot like Ann, too, come to think about it. Always kind of bounces when he walks and acts like everything is fun and exciting, without ever really saying so. Yeah, it adds up, all right.'

Levi stood, excitement beginning to build within him. He always felt that exhilarating lift when he caught the scent of his prey and began to close in. It had been a frustrating investigation. The frus- tration added to his excitement, as the feeling grew that he was close to a solution.

This time, there was an added element of excite- ment. If he could wrap up this investigation, he would be free to make plans for that life he had des- paired ever being able to live. He could begin to plan to have a wife. A home. Children. With the excite- ment putting an edge on his voice he said, 'I believe I'll ride out and have a talk with Mr Brickner.'

'You want me to go along?'

'No, I guess not. He's just one man. From what you say, he probably isn't very dangerous to anyone facing him.'

'Be careful.'

'Occupational habit, remember?' Levi smiled tightly as he walked out the door.

He stood in the gathering darkness pondering the situation for several minutes. Finally he said to himself, Guess it wouldn't be too smart to go blundering out there in the dark. I'll stay over and ride out early in the morning.

He went to his room at the hotel, rolled into bed, and was almost instantly asleep.

He smiled a contented welcome to the dreams that came.

FOURTEEN

The sun had not yet found the Wyoming sky when Levi rode out of Ten Sleep. He followed the main road east along the turbulence of Ten Sleep Creek. He rode swiftly, but alertly. He was already swinging toward the south by the time the morning sun climbed enough above the mountains to hamper his vision. He had ridden too many trails of danger to ride into the sun where he couldn't see clearly ahead of himself, and he did not do so now. By leaving the road and swinging to the south, then back east after the sun was high enough to present no hazard to his vision, he approached the Box-A ranch from the rear. He emerged from the trees less than fifty yards from the buildings.

It was early afternoon. The ranch yard lay in a peaceful haze in the warm sun. The drone of deer flies swarming around the body of a young bird, fallen from its nest, added to the depth of the silence. Levi sat still on his horse, unwilling to disturb the serenity of a perfect day. He faintly heard a splash as a trout leaped for some insect in a quiet pool of Meadowlark Creek beyond the yard. Leaves rustled as some tiny animal scurried about on business known only to itself. It was such an idyllic scene only Levi's experience kept him alert and poised for danger.

Seeing nothing out of the ordinary, he lifted the reins and goaded his horse to a slow walk. He approached the yard in a slow circle that would bring him into the yard by the main road. He was not yet around the corrals when Ann spotted him from the house. She ran from the porch and across the yard, calling to him.

'Levi! I was hoping you'd get back today!'

He turned his horse directly toward her and rode at a trot. He slid from the saddle as she neared, taking her in his arms and tasting the remembered sweetness of her lips. She clung to him for just a moment extra, then backed away, keeping her hand on his arm and smiling impudently.

'And just what do you mean by sneaking in through the timber?' she asked with a tilt of her head.

He grinned at her. 'Thought I'd sneak up and see who was makin' eyes at my girl, before I showed myself.'

'Oh, really! You mean I'm not even allowed to flirt with some poor lonesome cowboy?'

'Only if you want some lonesome cowboy beat up somethin' awful,' he replied, swatting in the general direction of her rear with his hat.

She yelped in pretended surprise and looped a clumsy kick at his shins. He kicked her planted foot out from under her while her other foot was still in the air. He caught her as she fell, squealing, toward him. 'Now there you go, falling for me again,' he said.

Striking a melodramatic pose with the back of her hand to her forehead, she said, 'Oh, handsome lawman, I couldn't help it, you just swept me off my feet.'

Laughing, they walked toward the house. Then the reason for his return intruded its unwelcome presence on Levi's mind. He turned to Ann in sudden seriousness. 'Sweetheart, I've got to talk to you. I've learned some things and I've got to talk about something I know you don't want to discuss. I think I know who's been doing all the killing.'

Her sharp intake of breath was the only indication she had heard him. He looped the reins of his horse over the hitchrail in front of the porch and followed her into the dim coolness of the house. Kate Banner greeted him. 'Well, hello, Levi. When did you get back?'

'Just now. Mrs Banner, would you please join us? I've got to talk with Ann about some things, and I'd appreciate it if you were there too. Is Tom around?'

She shook her head, probing his face for some reason for his seriousness and his request. 'He rode over to the Round Rock Hollow with Dusty, Jack and Snuffy to check that old bog hole. They might have to fence it off.'

'When do you expect them back?'

'Probably within another couple of hours, maybe less.'

He nodded. 'Could we sit down?'

Both women watched his face intently as he fished for words. Finally he asked, 'Ann, do you know anything about your mother's family?'

Ann's face blanched and her mouth tightened. Her eyes took on that flat emptiness he had only seen twice before. It deeply disturbed him, but he made no move to lift the question. Finally, speaking the words through tightly drawn lips and in distant tones, Ann replied, 'No. Why?'

As he spoke he reached to take one of her hands in both of his. 'Ann, I know this all has to bring up an awful lot of old hurt. I'm sorry. Everybody who has been murdered was in the bunch that killed your folks.'

Levi heard the sharp intake of Kate's breath, but his eyes never left Ann's face. He saw the fierce flash of fire that leaped from her eyes. He watched the obvious struggle as Ann fought for control, stifling an intense passion she had kept buried for so long, forcing it back down beneath the blank and empty blandness of her eyes. When she could control her voice, she spoke again, so softly he could scarcely hear her. 'What do you mean?'

'I mean someone is getting revenge for their deaths. We know your mother had a brother by the name of Clay Allison. He was wanted for murder in New Mexico and Texas, then later around Cheyenne. We think he eventually found out what happened to his sister, and has set out to get even.'

Ann's eyes darted back and forth from Kate to Levi. Once she looked like she was about to laugh, then like she would cry instead. Finally she whispered, 'You mean I have an uncle? He's here? You think he's doing all the killing? Who is he?'

Levi argued silently with himself for a long

moment before he answered, trying to determine whether it was wise to tip his hand this quickly. It was his heart that made the decision for him. 'I can't be sure yet,' he said slowly, 'but I think he's Dusty Brickner.'

Kate's gasp was so sudden and loud Levi jumped. An expression crossed Ann's face he could not fathom at all. It looked like a mixture of triumph and fear, and he had no idea how to interpret it. It was Kate who broke the silence. 'Dusty? But he's such a jolly hand, and such a good worker.'

Their conversation was interrupted by the sound of several horses entering the yard. Looking quickly out the window Levi saw Banner riding up, accompanied by Dusty and two other hands. Throwing a look of warning at the two women, Levi stepped out the door, lifting the thong off the hammer of his .45 as he did so.

The men dismounted in the yard, starting toward the barn with their horses. Tom Banner handed his reins to Snuffy and started for the house. He spotted Levi and stopped, warned by Levi's posture.

Levi moved to a point that separated Dusty from the others, giving the man no opportunity to use his horse as a shield. Drawing his pistol he spoke softly. 'Dusty, move your hands away from your gun and turn around.'

Confusion followed by a flash of anger crossed Dusty's face. He looked hard at the steady, uncompromising stare of Levi's Colt. Slowly he raised his hands and turned around.

Levi moved swiftly to slip Dusty's pistol from its

holster, then ran a practised hand around him for hidden weapons. From a sheath suspended between his shoulder blades he drew out a large, well-balanced knife.

'Mr Banner,' he called. 'Would you please grab the piggin' string off his saddle and tie his hands behind him?'

'What's going on, Levi?' Banner asked. 'Are you arresting this man?'

'I am. I'll explain when you get his hands tied.'

Still obviously confused, Banner complied. When the man's hands were firmly bound behind him, Levi exhaled slowly and holstered his own gun. All the hands had assembled, watching the proceedings with intense interest. Kate and Ann stood beside Tom, leaving Levi and Dusty isolated in the centre. Levi raised his voice.

'As a duly authorized deputy of Washakie County, I declare this man under arrest for the murder of six men.'

An excited buzz erupted from the assembled hands. A single voice rose above the rest. 'What makes you think Dusty killed 'em?'

'I have reason to believe his real name is Clay Allison, and that he is the brother of Ann's mother, a well-known and wanted outlaw in New Mexico. He came here under false pretences to learn the names of those involved in the killing of Ann's parents, and to kill them in revenge.'

The excited buzz of voices erupted again, then stopped abruptly when a man stepped out ahead of the others. 'You got a bum steer, Hill. I knowed Dusty's folks back in Nebrasky. He sure ain't Clay Allison.'

'I got to agree with that,' another hand intruded. 'I seen Clay Allison in Cheyenne one time. He was about Dusty's size, but he didn't look nothin' like 'im at all.'

Banner entered the discussion. 'Levi, I have to disagree too. Dusty couldn't possibly be the one. During the time Binder and McClatchey were killed, Dusty was laid up. His horse took a fall off a rimrock. He wasn't in any shape to kill a rabbit for a while there.'

Levi looked around at the circle of faces while he pondered everything that was being said. He kept looking back to Ann, but her face held an expression he couldn't begin to fathom. Finally the obvious occurred to him. He turned back to his prisoner. 'Dusty, I want you to walk toward Mr Banner.'

With his face showing his obvious lack of comprehension, Dusty complied, walking slowly and uncertainly. 'That's far enough,' Levi said when he had taken half a dozen steps.

He walked over behind Dusty and studied the ground. There were several perfectly formed footprints in the dust of the yard. In his mind Levi tried desperately to get any part of the outer curve of his track to fit his memory of that one smudged, partial track he had found. They were the wrong tracks. He sighed and walked to the younger man. 'Dusty, I owe you an apology. I got the wrong man. I thought I had it all figured out. Clay Allison is the man we want, but you ain't him.'

'If Clay Allison was around here, you'd have more'n six men dead,' the one who had spoken up before declared. 'That man leaves a whole string of dead men behind him. Why he even shot a man once just because he was snorin'!'

'Naw, that was Wes Hardin done that,' another hand argued.

The hands began to filter toward the bunkhouse. The air was suddenly filled with stories of famous gunfighters and killers, and with arguments about which inflated exploits belonged to which. Levi untied Dusty as quickly he could. He stepped back awkwardly while the cowboy rubbed his wrists. He took a step forward then, and extended his hand. 'Dusty, I'm sure sorry. I was wrong, and I made a fool of myself. I hope there's no hard feelin's.'

Dusty hesitated a moment, then took the extended hand. 'I'm just glad I was the wrong guy,' he said. 'Hangin' ain't my idea of a good way to die.' As the cowboy's relief faded, his anger returned, and he spoke. 'I will tell you this. I don't care if you are a lawman. If you ever accuse me of anything again, you better kill me, 'cause if you don't I'll kill you.'

He stamped off toward the bunkhouse, leaving Levi to stand awkwardly. More than his embarrassment in front of the Banners, he had made himself look foolish to Ann.

'Well!' Banner said, a bit too loudly and heartily. 'Let's go on inside and talk this over. You really think Ann's uncle is the one doing the killing?'

Ann moved to Levi and took hold of his arm with both hands. 'Levi, do we have to dig all that up? I haven't talked about it since it happened, and I don't want to have to talk about it now. I won't talk about it now!'

Levi laid his other hand on hers consolingly. 'I

know Ann, I know, but he's got to be stopped. There are six men left who are targets, and he won't quit till he kills them all. Ann, that includes Tom!'

The reaction he expected from Ann was not forthcoming. She just continued to look into his eyes with a deep pleading in her own. 'I just want to forget about it. Please?'

All he could think of to say was, 'I'm sorry,' and they walked on into the house. Something he was missing niggled at the corners of his mind. He just couldn't get hold of its substance. He knew it was important. His life might depend on it. But it stayed there, just out of his mind's reach. It poised, hovering above him, as though ready to snuff out his life. He just couldn't figure out what it was.

FIFTEEN

Levi's thoughts were still in turmoil when he rode out the next morning. Ann had refused to participate in the conversations about her parents' deaths and the presumed presence of her mother's brother. She had worn that same inimical expression that so confused him every time the subject of her parents was broached. It was only after the conversation moved on to other matters that her mood changed.

When her mood did change, it was as abrupt and startling as the sun emerging from behind a cloud. Almost instantly she was all smiles and laughter. After supper they had taken a walk along the edges of the timber west of the place. He wanted the night to never end.

As he saddled his horse this morning the memories of her closeness and the fresh smell of her hair flooded through him. Some of the tracks around the corral tugged at the corners of his mind, but he ignored it. He was lost in the headiness of his love.

He rode north and east, crossing Meadowlark Creek, angling directly toward the Marchant ranch. Ike Marchant was just riding out of the yard with two of his hands when Levi rode into sight. Levi rode directly to the trio.

'Fine morning,' he greeted.

'Sure is,' Marchant agreed. 'You'd be Levi Hill?'

'That's right,' Levi grinned. 'I visited with your wife the other day, but hadn't had a chance to meet you.'

The rancher extended a hand. 'My hands, Luke and Frazer,' the rancher said, indicating the others.

Levi shook hands with the two cowboys, then returned his attention to the rancher. 'I'm fishing for information. We finally got a line on who's been doing all the killing. We know his name, but don't know what he's going by, or looks like. Do you have a hand that hired on less than a year ago? Small man, maybe five-six, that nobody knew?'

Marchant thought about it for a moment. 'Naw, can't say as I do. That ain't really a small enough man to stand out though, but most of the ones that ride in lookin' for work been around the country. Ain't too many ride in that nobody knows. Only one I can even think of is the flunky on the McClatchey place.'

Levi nodded, pondering whether to tell Marchant anything more or how to do so. Finally he said, 'Ike, there's something more you got a right to know. You're most likely a target too. Every one who's been killed was in the bunch that rode up to Spencer's that time. The killing all looks like revenge. You were in that bunch, so that probably means you're marked for murder too.'

The rancher sat completely motionless, staring at Levi while the words soaked in. Finally he reached a hand to his forehead and pushed his Stetson up in front, so it rested farther back on his head. He folded both hands on the saddle horn and leaned on them. 'I hadn't made the connection, but you're right. Every man who's been killed was with us that day. You figure out who's doin' it?'

Again Levi hesitated briefly. 'Well, we can't be sure yet, but we figure it might be Clay Allison.'

The trio stiffened. They looked quickly back and forth, then back at Levi. 'What would a gunman like Allison have to do with it?' Marchant asked.

'Marie Spencer was his sister.'

'Then why'd he take this long to get involved?'

'Can't answer that,' Levi admitted. 'Might be he didn't know about it before. Seems they weren't very close. Ann didn't even know her mother had a brother.'

'That so? Well, if I was related to that mangy coyote I don't suppose I'd brag about it either. Now you figure he's working for somebody around here?'

'Don't know that either,' Levi shook his head. 'Just seems likely he'd hire on with somebody. He could let the bunkhouse gossip tell him who was involved. Then he could kill when he got the chance without tipping his hand.'

Marchant nodded thoughtfully. Finally he said, 'Well, I'll keep an eye out, and we'll see if we can think of anyone who'd fit the description. Thanks for the warning.'

Levi touched his hat brim and turned his horse,

heading back toward Ten Sleep. He headed toward the livery barn, but Marshal Hansen stepped out the door of his office and motioned him over. 'Tie up your horse and come on in,' he said, nodding at the hitchrail.

Levi looped the reins around the rail and walked into the office, sitting down across the desk from the marshal. 'I hit a dead end, Arlo,' he said, without waiting for the marshal to open the conversation. 'I arrested Brickner, but found out in one big hurry he's the wrong man. I ain't felt that stupid in a long time. I thought sure he was the right one when I searched him, though. Found a knife in one of them sheaths between his shoulders, so he could draw and throw it in one motion. That fitted so well with Binder having his throat cut.... Anyway, there was a hand there who knows Brickner's folks in Nebraska, and another one who knows what Allison looks like, and they both said Dusty ain't him. Banner says Dusty was laid up from a spill on his horse when two of the murders took place, so he ain't our man.'

The marshal held up a hand to stop him. 'If you'd quit runnin' off at the mouth for about a minute I could save you a lot of rambling. I got a wire back from New Mexico.'

'About Allison?'

'Uh huh. It seems Allison ended up being a respectable rancher down in Colfax County. He got himself killed about five or six years ago.'

'Killed?'

'Killed. Seems he fell off the wagon he was driving, and it run over his neck and killed him.'

Levi was incredulous. 'Fell off a wagon?'

The marshal chuckled. 'Sure does beat all, doesn't it? Him a man who's supposed to've killed upwards of forty men! He tried to catch a sack of flour or something that was falling, and fell off the wagon and got killed. Anyway, that leaves us clear back where we started.'

He turned a yellow piece of paper toward Levi. He read the words of the telegram over and over. Finally he wadded it up and threw it to the floor. 'So we still don't know one single thing!'

'Well, not quite,' the marshal disagreed. 'The connection is too strong to just be coincidence. We still know somebody is getting revenge for the Spencers. We just have to start over with trying to figure out who and why.'

Levi pondered it for several minutes, trying to bring some order into the chaos of his thoughts. 'Got any ideas?' he asked finally.

'Not really,' the marshal shrugged. 'The only one I've even thought of is maybe some cowboy that's all in love with Ann. A young fella that ain't just right in the head might decide he could win her heart by avenging her parents.'

Levi considered that for a long moment. 'That's a possibility. My first instinct is to go right back to Dusty Brickner, but it can't be him. Banner himself said he was laid up when two of the murders were done. Anyway, his foot just won't match that part of a track I found.'

They talked the matter over until he felt like a dog chewing the same tired old bone. He hung around town for two days, listening, talking, rehashing everything with the marshal. Late the second day he told the lawman, 'I'm going to ride out in the morning. I'm going to visit each of the ranches and homesteads again, and see if anyone has an idea who might be trying to even up a score that old.'

He really had no idea where to look. He just knew he couldn't sit around town any longer. Something kept niggling at the corners of his mind, but he couldn't get a grasp on it. That hovering menace also stayed at the edges of his awareness. He could not identify either one.

From too many years of danger, he knew such a mental block could be fatal. He could not have been more right.

SIXTEEN

'I ain't never been this jumpy for no reason.'

Something urgent crowded the corners of Levi's mind. It raised the hackles on his neck. It refused to go away. It proved equally impossible to identify.

He visited with three homesteaders as he passed their places. The westering sun found him close to the grove he had camped in, the night after he had unexpectedly encountered Ann riding alone. The memory of that afternoon settled across him like a fragrant mantle, and he decided to camp there again.

He fixed himself some supper over a small smokeless fire, then took his cup of coffee and walked to the place he had spent that afternoon with Ann. He sat down on a big deadfall log, savouring the coffee and the memory. He was still taken aback at the memory of her demanding fervour and almost frantic need for him. His eyes dreamily traced out their tracks and the crushed grass, reliving each precious moment. There had been no rain, and not even a heavy dew for the past week. The tracks were still as fresh as the day they were made.

Something about those tracks sent a barb through him, but he passed by it, smiling dreamily. The tracks pulled his eyes back again. Over the rim of his coffee cup, he studied them with the instinct of a tracker.

He smiled at Ann's tracks, more deeply impressed in front, where she had stood on her toes, reaching up to find his mouth with hers. He traced the tracks as he remembered how she had broken away and took three or four steps away, then turned around and rushed back to him. He started to trace the steps on from there, but his eyes kept pulling back to those tracks. Something about those prints demanded his attention, but he just couldn't get a handle on it.

As he looked at Ann's tracks, he remembered the intensity of his old loneliness, born out of the conviction no woman would ever have him. He had been so sure he was destined by some Higher Power to be a lone wolf. To be happy, to find love, had been no part of his destiny.

Now, for the first time in his life, those thoughts were all reversed. He had found someone who loved him! Even when he was not with Ann, the knowledge of her love filled him with a jubilant, buoyant happiness. He stood there, studying the tracks that spelled out his happiness, sipping on his coffee until the cup was empty.

Finally he flipped the grounds from the bottom of the cup onto the ground and turned away. He went back to his camp. Dousing his fire, he rolled into his blankets, falling asleep almost at once.

He had been sleeping almost an hour when he sat bolt upright in his blankets. His eyes were wide open, but unseeing. His jaw hung open, and his hands lay at his sides, palms up. He sat there staring at nothing for a full minute, his mouth gaping open motionlessly. Finally a single word whispered past the yawning portal. 'No!'

The whisper faded into the silence of the trees around him, then it was followed by another. 'No!'

He lunged from his blankets and plunged through the darkness to the place he had studied the tracks he and Ann had made. With the instinct of an outdoorsman he went directly to the place. From that spot, the tracks had reached into his sleep and called to him with a message he could not receive. He dropped to his knees. Striking a match, he cupped it so its flame would illuminate the ground. Moving about, he quickly found a single track from Ann's boot.

The match burnt his fingers and he threw it to the ground, cursing. He lit another, and studied the track in its dim and flickering light. There along the outer edge of her left boot track was that small irregularity he had seen in the killer's track!

Moving like a man in a daze he stood up, walked back to the log he had sat on earlier. He dropped heavily on to it, as though his weight was suddenly too much to keep upright. He rested his elbows on his knees and leaned forward, sitting motionless, staring into the darkness. Every few moments he whispered, 'No!' again.

The night was long. So long it seemed at last he had grown old, and a long life had passed. The weight of his pain pressed him downward. He felt he could never stand erect again. All through the night he kept rehearsing all the things he hadn't been able to see, because he was looking in the wrong direction, because he was blinded by love, by the impossible realization of a forbidden dream.

The sun was sending its scouting rays of light ahead, prying into the corners of the night's secrets when he finally started talking out loud to himself.

Ann is the only one that would want to get even for their deaths, he told himself. She can shoot like nobody I've ever seen. She could get behind Binder, if she was the one he was expecting for dinner. She could get as close to anyone as she wanted, without their ever getting suspicious. She told me herself, when we watched that sunrise, that there are some that need to die, and their deaths is a good thing, not bad. She won't talk about her folks. She ain't never gotten over it. She'd just pushed it down and let it fester inside her all these years. She just waited, till the Banners would let her start riding around alone. All those years, she just waited. It was her track! It was her who killed Gert Kaiser, and she was on her way home when she found me here. It wasn't me that got her so excited. It was 'cause she'd just killed another one.

A great sob racked him. He stifled it, continuing his one-sided conversation. It was just coincidence that she killed Kaiser while we still thought the killer might have been Malvern. She couldn't have known about that yet. But if she did know it, she'd have hurried up and killed another one anyway. It wouldn't do any good for her to get revenge, unless people could eventually figure out who was being killed and why. Maybe she figured that by the time they did, we'd be off somewhere, married with a batch of kids, and I'd never even know.

Then another thought struck him like a sledgehammer, a thought too horrible to think. He thrust it away, but it hammered back at him. He shuddered. Another great sob racked him. He finally put it into words. Or maybe she was just using my love to keep me off her trail.

Daylight was two hours old before he stirred from the log. When he did, he stood up like an old man. Stiff and bent, he took his first steps like a rheumatic old codger unable to bear his own weight. He stopped and looked around at the tracks again. Another great sob racked him. Biting his lip to stifle it, he stumbled to where he had pitched his camp. He picked up his rope, then found and caught his horse. He saddled up and loaded his gear, then rode slowly from the grove of trees.

He had ridden for over an hour before he realized he was still riding toward the Johnson ranch. When that realization struck him he stopped and sat on his horse, trying desperately to think rationally. Suddenly a single clear idea broke through. He grasped it as though it would rescue him from insanity.

'If I'm right,' he said softly, 'then Johnson's got to be on the list too. Wouldn't hurt to go ahead and talk to him. I don't know how she gets everybody she wants to kill off by himself, but I can guess. I've got to warn Johnson, if nothin' else.'

He really wasn't sure what he was riding to, at the Johnson ranch. Whatever it was, he was sure he didn't want to ride toward it. He wasn't sure he wanted to ride toward anything. Not any more.

SEVENTEEN

'You must be Levi Hill.'

Tillie Johnson was a short, heavy and homely woman, but her eyes were crinkled with good humour. Her cheeks were rosy with the heat and exertion of baking. She was wiping her hands on her apron. She pushed aside a wisp of hair from her forehead, leaving a trace of flour.

Levi nodded. 'My reputation seems to run ahead of me.'

She nodded, made cautious by his haggard appearance. 'Have you had dinner?'

He shook his head. 'No, but I really don't have time to stop just now. Is your husband around?'

The concern in her eyes deepened. 'Yes. Him and the boys are working on the breaking corral.'

He followed the direction she pointed, and saw a man and two nearly grown boys. They were just lifting a peeled pine pole into place on the side of a high corral fence just past the barn. Touching the brim of his hat to her, he said heavily, 'Thank you, ma'am,' and turned his horse away.

The three saw him coming and stopped their work to await his arrival. 'Howdy,' he said quietly as he approached.

'How'd do,' Johnson replied. 'Step down. Care for a drink of water?' he asked, motioning toward a bucket and dipper standing nearby.

'Thanks,' Levi said, realizing his thirst for the first time.

He walked to the bucket and drank deeply, flinging the last of the water from the dipper on to the ground and replacing it in the bucket. Turning back to the rancher he said, 'My name's Levi Hill. You've heard of me?'

The rancher nodded. 'I 'spect everyone in the country's heard of you. Glad to meet you. I'm Tommy Johnson. Folks call me Wink. These are my boys, Jedediah and Aaron.'

Levi nodded wordlessly to the two boys, then turned back to the rancher. 'I wonder if I might have a word with you, kinda private?'

The rancher's eyes shadowed with caution and concern. He turned to his boys. 'You boys run on up to the house. Tell your ma to put on the coffee pot.'

The two boys looked protectively at their father, then at Levi, then at each other. Then they shrugged their shoulders at almost the same instant and walked away.

'Fine-looking boys,' Levi commented as they walked away.

It was impossible for the rancher to keep the pride out of his voice as he responded, 'They are that.'

Turning back to Levi he said, 'You look like you got kicked in the gut by a snaky bronc. What can I do for you?'

Levi looked off into space for several heartbeats

before he even attempted to answer. Finally he just took the bull by the horns.

'Wink, I got to ask you a question. Has Ann Banner been ... talking to you lately?'

The rancher had no chance to conceal the red flush that shot from his neckline to his scalp, or to control the stammer in his voice. 'Ann? Talk ... talk to me? Why? What do you mean?'

'I mean, has she been ... seeing you?'

The rancher looked toward the house, then back at Levi, then off into the distance. His eyes returned to Levi, but couldn't stay there. His Adam's apple bobbed up and down several times. With one boot he scuffed a flat spot in the dirt, then looked toward the house again. Finally he looked straight at Levi. 'She's your girl, I hear.'

Levi nodded. 'She is. But that ain't why I'm askin'. I got to know if she's asked you to meet her someplace.'

At the last words the rancher's head shot up with a tell-tale snap. He swallowed again several times. Finally he said, 'Aw, I don't know what's the matter with me! I got a good wife. I got two of the finest boys a man could ever want. It's just that, well, here I am past forty years old, and the prettiest and sweetest little thing I ever knowed starts paying attention to me. I start comparing her to my fat wife, and, and, aw, I ain't got no excuse at all.'

His eyes sought Levi's again, and his voice took on an almost defiant tone. 'But I ain't done nothin' with her. I don't suppose I probably will, either, but I sure been dreamin'! Then when she asked me to meet her, well, there just wasn't no way I could refuse.'

Levi walked over to the corral fence. He put one foot up on the bottom pole and leaned against it, his arms folded across the pole at shoulder height. He stared into the distance wordlessly.

It was the rancher who finally broke the silence. As soon as he started to speak, it was like a dam had broken. Things too long held within, tumbled over each other to get out. 'First time she really paid me any attention was at a barn dance last fall. Me and the missus was there, and she just up and asked me if I was goin' to dance with her. The missus she said she didn't care, so I did. I 'bout got lost in them dark eyes of hers. After that she just seemed to show up wherever I happened to be, and we started talkin', friendly like. It wasn't long till I sorta found myself lookin' for an excuse to go where I thought she'd be.'

He paused for a while, then looked back at Levi. 'I guess I didn't even think about where it was leadin' till she up and kissed me. I guess I just thought I loved her like a daughter or a sister or something till then. But then I realized I was just plumb head over heels in love with that girl. I ain't been able to really think about much else since. I never understood, before, how a man could leave his family for some pretty young thing. I always thought a man that'd do that ought to be horse whipped. Or hanged. I guess maybe I still think so, but I just can't help myself!'

Levi finally stirred from the corral fence and faced the rancher. 'Wink, do you know who Ann is?'

'What do you mean?'

'Do you remember her folks?'

The memory clicked into place with a visible jolt. 'Well, sure, I always knowed who she was, but it never seemed too important. We all just sorta forgot she wasn't Banner's. Why?'

Levi took in a deep breath, until his chest felt like bursting, then let it out slowly before he continued. 'The murders I've been brought in to investigate ... every one of them were in the bunch that killed her folks.'

Johnson looked stunned. Levi allowed the silence to hang heavily while Johnson mentally counted off the murder victims, confirming the connection. When he saw the rancher had digested that information, he continued, 'We thought at first her mother's brother had come into the country to get revenge. His name was Clay Allison.'

Johnson replied, 'That Clay Allison? The gunfighter?'

Levi nodded. 'That's him. But we found out yesterday he was killed five or six years ago down in New Mexico, so it couldn't be him. Then Gert Kaiser was killed. I found part of a track there. It had a little nick on the edge of the boot sole. It was small enough I wasn't sure whether it was really on the boot, or part of the smudging of the track. Then I saw the same nick on Ann's track. That's when I put it together.'

Both men silently stared into the painful fragments of shattered egos and broken dreams for a long moment. It was, again, Levi who broke the silence. 'Anyway, if I'm right, you're next on the list. If she's asked you to meet her off somewhere, then it has to be to kill you too.'

Johnson turned belligerently toward Levi. 'No! Can't you understand? She loves me! Is that so hard to believe, that she could love a busted down old cowpoke like me?'

Trying vainly to control the trembling of his own voice Levi said, 'She says she loves me too. She says she's never been so happy as she is whenever she's with me, and that she doesn't ever want to live another day without me.'

Johnson looked at him in open-mouthed amazement. 'That's exactly the things she keeps saying to me! She says I'm different than all the young cowboys...'

'...and mature and she can talk about things with you that she's never told anybody else ... right?' Levi continued for him.

It was Johnson's turn to feel a sob of anguish and betrayal ripped painfully from the centre of his being. He turned away from Levi, his fists bunched tightly against his sides. When he had regained the control of his emotions, he said in a barely audible murmur, 'What do you want me to do?'

That was the question to which Levi had practised his answer, over and over, as he had ridden here. He said, without hesitation, 'I want you to tell me when and where you're supposed to meet her. Then I want you to show up like you're supposed to. I'll be there, hid, and we'll find out for sure whether I'm right.'

The rancher thought it over slowly. At last he straightened his shoulders and looked Levi fully in the eyes. 'All right. It may get me killed, if you're right, but that's sure no more than I deserve anyway. I'm supposed to meet her at that grove of aspens where there's a little spring on the west slope of the big hogback between Marchant's place and hers.'

Levi gasped as he realized that was the exact place he had camped last night – the very place she had led him, secure from chance discovery, the day she had killed Kaiser. He struggled desperately to control his emotions. 'When?' he croaked.

'Tonight. Just after dark.'

Levi nodded. 'I know the place. You go ahead. Don't say anything to alarm her. Just let it play itself out. I'll be listening, and I'll keep her from killing you if she tries.'

The rancher shot a look toward the house 'You goin' to tell the wife?'

'It sure ain't my place to do that. I'll be there tonight. You won't see me, but count on me.'

He walked back to his horse and rode from the yard. His shoulders slumped forward. His body sagged. He rode like an old, old man, shuffling through dry husks of dead dreams.

EIGHTEEN

Levi felt as though he were made of lead. Especially his heart. His chest hurt with its heavy beat. He wished, with every part of his being, that it would just stop, of its own accord, and end this pain.

It lacked an hour of dark when he hid his horse in a small copse. He was 200 yards up the hill from the grove that was his destination. He removed his boots and replaced them with a pair of moccasins from his saddle-bags. He checked the loads in his Colt, then the loads in his rifle. Glancing at the position of the sun he estimated the time till dark. With a telescope from his saddle-bag he carefully surveyed the country around and beyond the grove. He needed to be sure he could traverse the distance to its cover without detection. Satisfied, he replaced the telescope in the saddle-bag and set out.

He kept to whatever cover was available as he worked his way down the slope. He paused every few minutes to listen, intent upon reaching concealment before either of the parties to tonight's rendezvous arrived.

He reached the grove without incident. It was a

relatively small grove, but he knew he could see as well as hear from only a short distance. That made it imperative that he guess with some accuracy the location Ann would choose to meet Johnson. As hard as it was for his heart to accept, his mind said she would pick the same spot at which he, himself, had so recently felt the sweet nectar of her embrace.

Moving swiftly and silently through the trees and brush, he selected a thick clump of brush at the very edge of the same clearing. There was just enough light left for him to clearly make out the familiar spots, including the one where he had stared so long and hard at her tracks in the dirt before the truth penetrated the barrier of his love.

The memories bore down upon him, making him feel trapped and starved for air. Wild, erratic and impossible solutions to the dilemma flashed through his mind. Beneath the turbulence, though, there was a hard base of character that kept him on course, even against his own will. He could no more have walked away, nor turned aside from this night's painful duty, than he could have willed himself to stop breathing.

The tumult of his mind was becoming almost unbearable when he heard the soft footfalls of an approaching horse. Crouching silently he saw Ann riding slowly through the trees, heading unerringly for the clearing where he had posted himself. With a palpable ache he watched her dismount. She tied her horse to a convenient limb and smoothed her blouse and skirt. She walked over and sat down on the very log on which Levi had spent the past night in agony. There was a strange, cold smile on her face that Levi could not remember seeing before.

Darkness was only a near promise when he heard another horse's approach. The horse stopped at the edge of the trees, and a tentative voice spoke. 'Ann? Are you here?'

Ann stood up, but made no effort to move toward the voice. Instead she called out, 'Tommy? I'm right here.'

Levi heard Johnson dismount from his horse, and traced the sound of his steps as he walked quickly toward the clearing. As he emerged from the trees Ann lifted her arms and moved quickly toward him.

'Oh, darling!' she said softly. 'I was so afraid you wouldn't come!'

She reached her arms around his neck and lifted her face hungrily. They locked in a passionate embrace for what seemed to Levi like an eternity. Through a roaring in his ears he heard Johnson saying, 'Oh, Annie, Annie, I've been such a fool! I don't care what anyone says, honey, I love you! I can't even work any more for thinking about you! You are so beautiful.'

She silenced the torrent of his words with her mouth. In the middle of their embrace she flinched. She gave a soft muted cry, then twisted slightly away from him.

'What's the matter?' he asked.

Affecting a sultry pout she said, 'Your gunbelt bruised me.'

As she said it, she rubbed a spot just inside the front of her hip bone like it was tender. He held up a hand. 'Just a second. I'll get rid of it.'

As he spoke, he unbuckled the belt and removed it. Wrapping the belt around the gun and holster, he turned and laid it aside on the ground. Ann watched silently. Levi noted, with an ache in his chest, the excited lift of her breasts against the front of her blouse. Johnson turned back to her.

'There, now. That better?'

She came into his arms again and once more found his mouth with hers. When she pulled back she let her hands slide down his arms and take hold of his hands. She moved his hands to the front of her blouse and said, 'Anyway, you don't need a gun, you know. You can have anything you want without it.'

The rancher grinned foolishly, his mind and hands equally full of the feel of her. He was capable of seeing and hearing nothing in the world except his aroused desire.

As though he was separate and above the intolerable pain he was feeling, Levi saw, through the gathering gloom, Ann's hand slip to the pocket of her skirt. It came out again with a double barrelled .44 derringer. The softness and desire was totally gone from her voice when she spoke.

'Take your filthy hands off me, you slimy two-timing snake-in-the-grass!'

Johnson froze like he had been stunned with a club. He stood there, his hands still poised in front of her, staring. 'What did you say?'

'I said, get your hands off me, you filthy pig!' she snarled.

'But, but, you said … I don't understand! What's the matter? Did I say something?'

'Do you know who I am?' she demanded, her

voice slapping like the flat crack of a rifle.

'Who are you? Of course I know who you are. You're Ann Banner! You're the girl I love! What's the matter with you?'

'I am not Ann Banner,' she spat back at him. 'My name is Ann Spencer, and you murdered my parents.'

'What? You mean, you mean ... it's true?'

Levi heard the realization flooding into the man's voice even though he could no longer see his face. Soundlessly he slipped from the brush of his concealment and began working his way behind Ann, even as he listened.

'You bet it's true, you murdering coyote! It's true that my parents were nothing but honest homesteaders. It's true that you ranchers were so greedy for every speck of land in the country you just had to keep crowding and crowding. When you couldn't crowd him off the land you came to our house on some trumped-up pretext and shot them in cold blood. I've waited years to get old enough and wise enough to make things right. Now you're all going to pay for what you did to my parents.'

'You, you mean it's you who killed all those men?' Johnson asked, still reluctant to believe.

Her laughter slapped Levi like a blow as he heard her answer. 'Who else in this country cares enough to see justice done? And you! You came here tonight thinking you were going to two-time your wife, so you doubly deserve to die like the pig you are. Die, like my parents died!'

Levi had moved unheard right up behind the raving girl. As she raised the gun to fire he grabbed her wrist, forcing the shot to go off harmlessly into the air. The second barrel discharged almost at once from her struggle to bring it to bear on her unexpected attacker.

As she squirmed in his grip, Ann twisted enough to see Levi. She relaxed abruptly. 'Oh, Levi! Oh, darling! I'm so glad you're here. Oh darling, he lured me here with promises of information that I could give you, and then he tried to rape me! Oh, darling!'

She wilted against him as though she was about to faint, but he jerked away from her. His voice was taut with intensity. 'Give it up, girl! I've been listening the whole time. Ann, I'm sorry. You can't possibly know how much this hurts me, but you are under arrest for murder.'

'What? Darling you can't mean that!' she said, with every appearance of offended innocence. 'Surely you can't mean that! You can't think I lied about how much I love you. Doesn't our love mean any more than that?'

'His love?' Johnson injected bitterly. 'I thought it was our love.'

'It's no use, Ann,' Levi said harshly. 'It took a long time for me to see it, just because I was dumb enough to love you so much. When I finally realized it was your track I found at Gert Kaiser's murder, I knew it had to be you.'

'Track?' Ann asked. 'There was no track! You can't trick me that way! There was no track left there at all!'

'Yeah, there was,' Levi disagreed. 'And it was yours. I didn't have any evidence that would stand in court, though, until tonight. That's why I told

Wink to come ahead and keep your rendezvous. I was sure you'd let him know why you were killing him before you did. There wouldn't be any satisfaction in it, otherwise.'

'Oh yes there would!' she spat. The façade of her pretences fell away, and her words dripped with hatred and venom. 'It doesn't make any difference how or when I see one of that murdering pack die, or whether they know or don't know. Caulder never knew! He just kept looking around like he couldn't imagine anyone ever wanting to hurt him. Neither did Wade Renfro, and I enjoyed his death just as much as I did Gert Kaiser's. And then, when I killed Kaiser, you showed me how to really celebrate the victory over one of my parents' killers.'

Levi could not stand to hear any more. 'Shut up!' he barked, and pulled her arm down and around behind her. He looped it with the pigging string he pulled from his back pocket, then pulled the other arm around and bound them together behind her back.

'Do you have to do that?' Johnson asked.

'Absolutely,' Levi answered without hesitating. 'Most lawmen who get killed, get killed by a prisoner they didn't think they needed to tie up. I'll be asking you to ride into town with me. I'll need your word too, when we turn her over to the marshal.'

Johnson looked like he was about to offer several protests, but then his shoulders sagged and he said, 'Least I can do, I guess. You did save my life.'

Levi hoisted Ann to her saddle, took the reins

and led the animal from the clearing. They walked together to Johnson's horse, then back up the hill to where Levi had hidden his own. There was no other word spoken by any of the three throughout the long ride in the darkness. The night that surrounded each of them was a lesser gloom than each felt within. The only protection from the intolerable pain any of them could find was a wall of silence.

NINETEEN

It was not quite daylight when the despondent cavalcade plodded slowly into Ten Sleep. They stopped beside the marshal's office. Levi dismounted and just raised his hand to knock when the door opened before him. The marshal, clad in long underwear and holding a gun in his hand, squinted into the dark.

'Prisoner?' he grunted.

Levi nodded woodenly. 'It's done, Arlo.'

'Bring him in. Then you can tell me about it.'

Levi turned back to Ann. He grasped her by the waist, lifting her easily from the horse, and stood her on the ground before him. The smell of her hair caused the intolerable ache to leap up within him again. As he guided her to the door he was vaguely aware of Johnson dismounting behind him.

The old habit of wariness stabbed through his grief and fatigue. He stepped quickly around Ann to face back toward the rancher. Johnson was standing beside his horse, hand on his gun as though an imponderable battle was waging within him. He heaved a heavy sigh and pushed away from his horse. His hand fell away from his gun, and Levi relaxed again, almost staggering with the release of tension.

The marshal turned from lighting a lamp. His mouth dropped open until it threatened to engulf his great moustache. His eyes darted from Ann to Levi to Johnson to Ann again. Finally finding his voice he said in an offended tone, 'What's this, Levi? You arrested ... you, you arrested ... her? Ann? Why?'

Levi sagged against the wall. 'It's a long story, Arlo. Please take the ropes off her and lock her up. It'd be advisable to have your wife check her for weapons. I didn't search her.'

The marshal looked belligerently back and forth from one of them to the other. He saw the pain in their faces, as well as Levi's fatigue. He recoiled from the force of venom stabbing from Ann's eyes. He chewed the corners of his moustache, then turned toward the door to his living quarters. 'Maudy,' he called. 'I need your help.'

A few minutes later the marshal's ample wife emerged from their quarters. 'Why, Ann,' she said, 'whatever is this all about?'

'Maudy, I'll be needin' you to check her over for weapons. We'll hang blankets around the cell by itself so she's got some privacy. Then we'll get our answers.'

Maude looked at the trio again, then at her husband. She nodded with a look that meant she would do as he asked, but she expected some answers in a hurry when it was done.

As the marshal and his wife took her through the door into the jail area, Levi collapsed into a chair. Johnson continued to stand just inside the door. Both men stared, mutely and disconsolately, into nothing.

A quarter hour later Arlo and Maude returned. The marshal sat down behind his desk, never thinking to offer his wife a chair. She stood with her arms folded, looking like she was about to spank the three of them.

'Well, she's as comfortable as she's likely to get in a cell. Now suppose you tell me just what this is all about.'

'She's the killer,' Levi said. 'She's just stored the killing of her folks down inside all these years. She had to wait till she was old enough until the Banners let her ride off by herself. She just waited, all those years, and never said a word. It was a part of her track I found where Gert Kaiser was shot. It didn't register for a long time, because I wasn't thinking of finding the killer when I was with her at all. I just wasn't doin' my job, Arlo.'

'Well, you best start from the very first and fill me in,' the marshal said with a harsh edge on his voice. 'Then I'll decide whether to believe you or lock you up instead.'

Leaving out nothing, Levi retraced his reasoning up to the point that he confronted Johnson. At that point he looked at Wink, who only nodded his head. Levi noticed a lone tear that had escaped his control. It slowly ploughed a furrow through the dust on his face.

Turning his eyes back to the marshal, he completed the story as quickly as possible. He included the way in which Ann had used the promise of her body to remove Wink's gun. He related the things she had told Johnson when she anticipated killing him. He finished with a helpless lift of one hand, that fell back limply to the arm of his chair.

The marshal turned the whole story over and over in his mind. 'Well! Don't that beat all!' he said, finally. 'We had it all figured out except who was doing it. We just never even thought of the most obvious one, just because she's a woman.'

'Because she's a very pretty woman,' Maude corrected. 'If she were an ugly old crone it would be much more believable, even for me. But she's so pretty and bright and has a pleasant way about her. Land sakes! It sure does beat all!'

'It sure does beat all!' the marshal echoed. When the silence again hung heavily in the air, he said, 'It sure does beat all.'

'Who's going to tell the Banners?' the marshal's wife asked suddenly.

The question hung there in the air, begging an answer nobody wanted to offer. It was Levi who finally spoke. 'I guess I'll have to,' he said reluctantly.

'You don't look to me like you're in any shape for another ride that far,' the marshal said.

'I'll make it,' Levi said as he rose to his feet. 'When does the circuit judge come to town?'

'Next week, as fate would have it,' the lawman said. 'Probably a good thing, too. This ain't somethin' I want to drag out any.'

'I'll be back to town in a day or two,' Levi said. 'When word gets out, there may be trouble.'

'Most trouble is likely to be for you,' the marshal growled. 'Some love-struck cowboy's bound to take a pot shot or two at you for arresting her, not to mention that they'll all think your name's Judas.'

'I guess it is,' Levi said softly, as he shuffled to the door. 'You plannin' to ride back home, Wink?'

The rancher looked at him like he just awakened suddenly, and wished he hadn't. 'Yeah. I'll ride along with you to the Box-A fork.'

The two men walked together to their tired horses. They took Ann's horse to the livery barn. They had to forcibly urge their own mounts to leave the welcome haven of rest and feed. They let them drink at the water trough, then pushed them out of town toward the mountains looming in the east.

They rode in silence for nearly an hour, each lost in the morass of his own emotions. Johnson finally spoke. 'What am I goin' to tell her?'

'Who?'

'My wife.'

'I don't know. Why not tell her the truth?'

'I can't hurt her like that! She's a good woman, Hill. She's stood by me, good years and bad, all down the line. She fought a timber fire beside me one time, when she was heavy with child. She's backed me against Indians, when a band of roving renegades come through. She's given me two fine sons. She ain't pretty, but she's a fine woman!'

'You shoulda thought of that before.'

'If I told her what Ann was up to, and that you asked me to string along with her, like you did, would that be lyin'?' Johnson asked.

Levi considered it. 'Well, I guess it ain't exactly lyin'. 'Course, it ain't exactly bein' honest, either.'

'I know that,' Johnson said, with a pained

expression. 'And I expect she'll figure out maybe I wasn't too innocent, but maybe she'll kinda let it slide. Then I can make it up to her, somehow.'

Little more was said until the trail to the Box-A turned off. They stopped and looked at each other for a long moment. It was, again, Johnson who spoke first. 'Well, I'll see you later. I reckon we'll both have to be there for the trial.'

'Yeah,' Levi sighed. 'That ain't gonna be easy either.'

There seemed nothing more to say, so he lifted his hand and turned his horse toward the Box-A. Another hour later he rode, swaying in the saddle, into the yard. He slid off the horse in front of the house, and didn't even bother to loop the reins over the hitchrail. The exhausted horse stood, spraddle-legged, his head hanging nearly to the ground. Snuffy walked over. 'That horse looks as done in as you do. Want me to rub 'im down and put 'im up for you?'

Levi straightened with an effort, a feeling of gratitude flooding through him. 'I'd sure be obliged, Snuffy. Are Tom and Mrs Banner both in the house?'

The old cowboy nodded. 'Tom ain't come out after dinner. They're some worried. Ann, she didn't come home last night. They figure as how she might be with you. You know where she is?'

Unable to speak, Levi just nodded. When he could trust himself, he choked out the words, 'She's in town,' and forced his legs to climb the steps to the porch.

Tom had heard the sound of voices and was just coming out the door as Levi stepped on to the porch. 'Levi! You look a sight! Come on in and sit down. Have you seen Ann?'

Levi nodded and walked into the dim coolness of the house, removing his hat as he stepped through the door. Kate stood just inside, looking at him worriedly. Levi walked into the kitchen and collapsed on to a chair, waiting for them to sit down before he began his story.

When they were set and he could think of no way to delay any longer, he forced himself to begin. 'I ain't had no sleep for two nights, so I ain't thinkin' and talkin' just the best, but I wanted to get here before anyone else did. I didn't want anyone else telling you what I got to say.'

'What's wrong, Levi?' Kate asked. 'Is it Ann?'

Levi nodded and swallowed several times before he was able to speak. His voice cracked when he said, 'She's in jail. It was her that's been killing people.'

Silence exploded into the kitchen, isolating it from everything else in the universe. It rotated slowly in an orbit of stunned disbelief. Its vacuum allowed no questions, no answers. It cradled only the shattered fragments of three people's world, exploded into jagged shards of pain.

Levi started to begin his explanation, in the words he had practised in his mind all the way from town, but that stifled sob ripped loose from its restraints and roared up from the white-hot core of his soul's agony. It issued from his mouth in a roaring sob that loosed an avalanche of grief. He tried in vain to staunch the flow of it, but he was too tired, too deeply hurt. He collapsed into a tearful heap, face buried in his arms on the kitchen table. Neither Tom nor Kate interfered or moved until his grief subsided and his control returned.

'I'm, I'm sorry,' he stammered, 'bawlin' like a baby. I'll get a rope on it in a minute.'

The rancher and his wife both watched him and waited in silence. Their mouths were drawn into tight lines. Tears were streaming down Kate's face, as she waited for the explanation she didn't want. Tom's eyes were dry, but they reflected the fear and pain that he was about to hear something that was going to do more than break his heart.

When he could trust himself to talk, Levi started at the beginning, filling them in on the whole story. The only response from either of them from start to finish was an 'Oh, poor Tillie!' that was torn from Kate's lips when he outlined Johnson's role in the story. Otherwise they listened in stoic silence, but Levi could hear their souls rip apart, thread by thread, as the story unfolded. When he finished he collapsed into silence, too spent to move or feel.

They all sat without moving until they were aroused by the sound of a running horse plunging into the ranch yard. Dusty's voice shouted, 'Tom, Tom, they got Ann in jail! Tom!'

Banner stepped stiffly to the porch to meet him. Dusty took one look at his face, and stopped so quickly he nearly fell. Banner spoke in a clear voice, with only the measured tread of his words testifying to the tightness of his control over himself. 'I know that, Dusty. I also know why. You tell the hands I will brook no efforts to interfere with the law. They are to stay completely out of it, and let the law handle the matter.'

Dusty looked at him in stunned disbelief. 'You mean you ain't even goin' to try to help her?'

'I will help her, however I can,' Banner assured him, 'but it will not be by a mob of angry cowboys riding to her rescue. You tell the rest of them I said that.'

He wheeled back into the house and spoke to his wife. 'Where's Levi?'

'I made him go up to bed,' she said. 'He was out on his feet. We can talk to him more when he wakes up.'

Banner reached for his wife. She came into his arms, and they stood there, locked in each other's embrace, sobbing into the void of each other's inconsolable grief.

TWENTY

'Looks like the fourth of July or something.'

'Worse than that,' the livery stable hostler growled back at Levi. 'Dangdest thing I ever saw. There's people ridin' in from Buffalo and Thermopolis and everywhere. I don't know how word could get around that fast.'

Dusk was settling on to Ten Sleep. The hitch rails along the street were filled with horses. Wagons and buggies filled virtually every available space.

Levi walked to the hotel and stopped at the desk. There was a cluster of people in front of it, all clammering at the desk clerk at once. He shrugged and ascended the stairs, hoping the harried clerk hadn't moved his stuff out and rented his room.

His things were undisturbed. He washed at the basin, filling it with water from the pitcher, then flinging the water from the window when he was finished. He didn't even look to be sure there was no one below when he threw it. He didn't care. He dressed in clean clothes and went back downstairs.

He spotted Tom and Kate Banner in the lobby,

talking with another rancher Levi remembered as Ike Marchant. He approached them, watching them stiffen as he neared. Noting the coldness in their eyes and expressions, he made no effort at light conversation. 'You see Ann?' he asked.

Tight-lipped, Tom nodded. 'She wouldn't say much to us. The marshal says she hasn't said a word to nobody but him.'

'She's talked to him?'

'So he says. He says she won't say nothin' except they all deserved to die.'

When Levi offered no response, he spoke again. 'Maybe they did. Maybe she had a right to kill 'em.'

It was Levi's turn to feel his lips press into a tight line. 'Includin' you? You're on that list too.'

Shock and surprise leaped into Banner's eyes. 'You mean you think she'd have killed me too? After all I done for her? Good Lord, man, that girl's like my own child!'

'To you she is. I ain't sure how she thinks at all.'

He strode out of the hotel and down the street to the marshal's office. He knocked at the barred and silent door.

'Who is it?' the marshal's voice demanded.

'Hill.'

The bar scraped from its brackets almost immediately, and he opened the door and stepped in. The marshal shut the door behind him, dropping the bar back into place. Levi eyed the bar questioningly.

'You expecting a jail break?'

'Already been two tries,' the marshal confirmed. 'I'm glad to see you back.'

'Two tries?' Levi asked, incredulous.

The marshal nodded. 'Just a couple or three drunk cowboys each time, but there'll be more.'

'What makes you think so?'

'Use your head,' the marshal growled. 'Half the country's in love with that woman. When a cowboy's lonesome and in love, it doesn't make any difference who she is or what she's done. He's just sure if he takes her away from here she'll love him forever.'

'When's the judge comin'?'

'Day after tomorrow, and a good thing, too. I can't keep a lid on this town any longer'n that.'

'You got any extra deputies?'

'Two. The sheriff's sendin' two more over from Worland. All told, that's seven of us, but seven ain't very many if somebody gets a bunch of drunks started up.'

Levi nodded. He stared at nothing, frowning, for several minutes. 'I'd just as well get my stuff from the hotel,' he said. 'Be better if I just camp over here.'

'Can you stand to be that close to her?' the marshal asked softly.

Levi's brows shot up, surprised again by the man's sensitivity and understanding. He shrugged. 'I'm so full of her inside, it don't matter whether I'm here or there.'

There was a long silence between them, then he asked, 'Can I see her, Arlo?'

The marshal looked at him a long moment, then nodded. 'Have to ask you to leave your gun here, o' course.'

Levi nodded and shucked his gun on to the

desk. He walked with dragging feet toward the door leading to the cells in the back of the building. The marshal unlocked the door, and he heard it lock again behind him.

At the end of the hall there was a single cell on one side. The other cells were all on the opposite side, making that one appear isolated, even if it wasn't. It had blankets hung from the inside of the bars, shutting it away from the eyes of other prisoners, should there be any. At the moment there were none.

Levi walked to the blanketed cell and spoke softly, a catch in his voice. 'Ann? You there?'

The blanket opened in front of him at once, and Ann faced him silently. He caught his breath sharply at the change three days had wrought. The laugh crinkles were gone from the corners of her eyes, replaced by others that seemed to pull her brows down menacingly. The dancing lights he loved to watch in her eyes were replaced by a single spark, boring like a focused beam from beneath the brows. Her lips were thin and pressed together. When she spoke her voice was flat and hard.

'Of course I'm here! Did you think they'd let me go to supper?'

'Would you have killed Banner too?' he blurted.

'Why wouldn't I? What did he ever do for me, except murder my parents?'

'But he took care of you! Raised you! Loved you!'

The spark blazed in her eyes. She almost spat the words, 'Took care of me? He wouldn't have needed to, if he hadn't murdered my parents. He did nothing for me! It was all just to try to ease his own conscience. They're all murderers!'

He didn't mean to blurt out his feelings, but they would be held no longer. 'But I love you!' he said.

The feverish fire of her expression abruptly and totally changed. 'Oh, Levi,' she said, reaching for him through the bars. 'Oh, Levi, take me away from here. I couldn't help it darling! I really didn't want to kill anybody, but every time I saw one of the men I knew was there, I just couldn't help what came over me. Just take me away from here! Take me away and let me love you! You'll never be sorry! I promise, I'll make you the happiest man in the world. Nobody will ever have to know who we are or where we came from! You can do it. You can find a way to get me out.'

The abrupt change left him stunned, then appalled, then he felt his iron façade begin to melt. The promise in her eyes twisted him. Law, honour, duty, all faded to abstract ideas, some place beneath and far away from the love that pulsed within him. He swallowed, not trusting himself to speak. He willed himself not to reach through the bars for the tender embrace she offered through the barrier.

In the confusion of turbulently mixed emotions he caught her reaching hands and grasped them in his own. 'Ann, Ann, I can't! I can't! I don't even have the keys!'

'You can get them!' Her eyes shone. 'The marshal can't stop you. You can take anything you want from him. We can go away, Levi, and put all this behind us, and forget it. It will never be able to interrupt our happiness and our love again.' Her voice turned husky with desire. 'Oh, Levi, I love you! I need you! I want you!'

Levi felt with shame the tears that escaped to run down his cheeks. With a greater shame he felt the weakening within himself. His resolve was melting. His hunger for her defied the logic of his mind. The loneliness he had felt through countless nights was too great. The impossible dreams that had suddenly become so possible were too alluring. He hated himself, because he was afraid she was only manipulating him, and he knew she was going to succeed.

He suddenly knew it, with utter certainty. He was going to free her. He was going to ride away with her. He was going to leave his decency and pride and self-respect in the shambles of the law, just for the sheer joy of holding her close to himself once more. The price he had to pay no longer made any difference. If it cost him his life, and the lives of all he cared about, it would be worth it, just to feel her arms around him, the fire of her lips.

Then another thought sprang, full-grown, into his mind. She might be right! Maybe it had been a planned attack to get her parents' land. Maybe it was murder, too long unavenged.

Sweat broke out on his forehead. His ears roared. His knees felt weak. A sharp rap on the door brought him crashing back to reality. He wheeled and lunged for the marshal's office. 'Levi, don't go!' she cried at his retreating back. 'Don't leave! Get the keys! I need you!'

The door opened just as he reached it, and he stepped out quickly. He sank into the chair behind the marshal's desk, sweating profusely. He buried his face in his hands, trembling all over. The marshal waited in silence for several minutes. 'Just about gave her too long, didn't I?' he asked softly at last.

Levi's head jerked up. 'You knew what she'd say?'

'Stood to reason,' the lawman shrugged. 'That's why I wouldn't let Tom and Kate talk to her alone. I don't think Tom could handle that, much less Kate. As long as I'm standing back a ways where she can see me, she knows better than to try it. She's a smooth one, that girl! Sure don't see how I could know her all these years and never see it.'

'She must be crazy,' Levi said softly, wiping again at the sweat pouring from his face. 'Seeing her folks killed like that must have done something inside her head.'

The marshal nodded sadly. 'In a way, I suppose that's probably right,' he said. 'I always said that anyone that killed others in cold blood had to be sort of crazy, some way. On the other hand, she sure knew what she was doing, and she sure knew it was wrong.'

'Are you sure?' Levi asked, as though a new idea had just dawned on him. 'Are you sure she knew it was wrong? Are you sure she didn't think it was the right thing to do?'

Hansen shook his head somberly. 'If she didn't know she was doing wrong, she wouldn't have been so careful to hide it. She was even willing to let you arrest Dusty for doing it.'

Levi started to protest that he knew she would never have let Dusty hang for the crime, but he bit his lip instead. He rose from the marshal's chair and paced the office for a long while in silence.

Finally, he said, 'I'll go get my stuff.'

The marshal shook his head. 'I reckon maybe it'd be best for you to stay at the hotel. Stay away till the trial. I hate to even ask you, but I'll need your help then. The day of the trial we'll need a pretty good show of force, so you bring whatever artillery you got.'

Levi nodded. He returned to his hotel in a daze.

The next day was uneventful except for a pervading sense of impending doom. He could not shake the feeling that something unforeseen was about to happen, and that it bode ill for him. It bode even worse than he had already been through, but he had no idea what could be worse. He became increasingly jumpy as the day progressed.

The judge drove his buggy into town late that afternoon. Notice was served to the owner of the Big Horn Saloon that he would be closed the following day, so the barroom could be used as a court. The air of expectancy, and the sense of foreboding raised to a palpable level.

The trial itself was little more than a formality. Ann readily admitted to the murders. The judge made a flowery speech about truth and justice for all. Then she was sentenced to be hanged, the following morning, at sunrise. Levi knew with certainty the whole town would turn out.

He also knew he was the only one that could keep it from happening.

TWENTY ONE

The world was too still to sleep, too small to hold his pain. A full hour before daylight Levi tapped at the marshal's door. It opened at once, and he looked down the barrel of a twelve gauge shot-gun. The gun barrel swung quickly aside, and Hansen said, 'Come on in, Levi. See anything out of the ordinary coming over?'

'Nope. Everything looks pretty quiet, but there's a lot of people out. There's already about fifty people up there by the tree. They act like they're afraid they're going to miss something.'

The marshal nodded. 'Some of them will ride twenty miles to watch a hangin',' he said, 'but there ain't half a dozen that'll even walk across the street to watch a second one. It is one God-awful thing to have to see!'

Levi nodded, still not trusting himself to speak more than necessary.

As Ann was brought from her cell he slowly lifted his eyes to look into hers. Her face was ashen. Her dark eyes looked twice as large as normal. Her hair was dishevelled, but she was still beautiful beyond words. Levi felt an overwhelming urge to say something, anything.

Finally he blurted, 'Ann, I'm sure sorry. I figured we'd spend the rest of our lives together, I, I....'

He turned away, unable to either look at her any longer or speak. When he turned back, her eyes were filled with silent pleading that needed no words. He knew what she was asking, and in that instant he knew there had to be some way to accomplish her release. He knew again with cold certainty he would find it. That image from last night's dream returned to his mind. He had felt her presence beside him, pressing against him, and felt the glow of pride in watching their children at play. Their children! He had seen their children! It was all in a dream, but he had seen their children! He had to make it real!

Another tap at the door broke the spell. The marshal swung it open, shot-gun again ready. It was Emmett, one of the special deputies sent from Worland to provide security for the trial. 'I got her horse,' he said.

Silently the marshal motioned them out, and the small procession moved into the street. The other deputy from Worland lifted Ann into the saddle. Levi noted he was shackled to her with a long chain. A local deputy held the horse's lead rope. Levi's practised eye picked out three deputies on the rooftops between them and the edge of town.

Like a fleck of metal to a magnet, his eyes were drawn to the big tree. It had already been, he knew, the scene of many hangings, and it stood as the town's symbol of law and order. A quiet voice in the back of his mind whispered, 'It must be cheated of its prey this day!'

At the marshal's word the procession started. Levi noted that every deputy carried a shot-gun in addition to his usual weaponry. The thought gave him a sudden qualm. It would make Ann's rescue a great deal more difficult.

They moved without incident to the big tree. A rope with a noose had already been thrown over the large limb that jutted horizontally from the trunk, nearly ten feet from the ground. The deputy with the lead rope led the horse to a position directly below the limb and stopped.

Another deputy on horseback rode up beside Ann, slipped the noose around her neck, and pulled it slightly snug. Ann flinched from the coarse bite of the rope.

As though it were all in slow and silent motion, Levi watched the proceedings. He saw Tom and Kate Banner standing at the edge of the crowd. Tom was staring at Ann as though he couldn't tear his eyes away, but Kate kept her face buried in her husband's shoulder. Her body shook with uncontrollable sobs.

Levi took a careful fix on the position of each deputy. He mapped out his plan of action in his mind. The first shot from his revolving shot-gun must be to sever the rope above Ann's head. He must wait until the deputy at her side was no longer shackled to her, so she could flee at once when he fired and yelled to her. Then he must shoot each of the deputies in the order of their threat to him. He would not have enough shots in the shot-gun, but the three on rooftops were out of shot-gun range anyway.

There were a lot of guns in the crowd that came

to watch, too, he knew. He also knew that at least half of them were hoping against hope that something would happen to stop the hanging. He knew some of them would do whatever they could to help their escape.

He fixed the position of the other deputy who was mounted. It would be necessary to kill him as one of the first ones, in order to have his horse for his own getaway.

Over and over Levi rehearsed in his mind the exact moves he must make, so that he could play out the entire desperate script without a least moment's hesitation. It was all such a closely timed thing that any deviation would mean his instant death, and probably Ann's as well.

He also knew that once the deputy and the rope imprisoning Ann were released, she would have a reasonable chance of escape. Nobody else except the one deputy was mounted. She would be able to put a good bit of distance between herself and any pursuit before it could be organized.

It was time. The marshal was returning. Everyone was watching either Ann or the judge. The deputy shackled to Ann was released. The chain was removed from Ann's wrist.

Levi looked up at Ann's face, and found her eyes searching his. There was something in his face that telegraphed his intention to her. Her eyes flared with a sudden impossible hope. She shot him a look that contained promises as old as the world – promises only a woman could offer the man she loved. Levi felt his heart soar. In that instant he knew himself capable of anything for the woman he loved.

He eyed the rope above her head again. His fingers tightened on the fire power of his revolving shot-gun. He tensed his muscles for action. He ran the sequence of moves through his mind again.

'A civilized country must have laws,' the pompous intoning of the judge began. He was repeating part of his speech from yesterday. 'If we are to be a civilized people, then lives must be protected by laws, not by guns and strength of hand. If laws are to be respected, then they must be fairly and impartially enforced, by men of integrity and honour.'

The steady drone of the judge's overly officious intonations faded into the background as Levi readied for action, but the judge's first words kept buzzing around in his head. 'A civilized country must have laws … men of integrity and honour. A civilized country must have laws....'

Unbidden, the words of the oath he had taken replayed themselves in his mind. 'I swear to uphold the laws of the Territory of Wyoming and the constitution of the United States of America....'

'A civilized country must have laws.... I swear to uphold the laws … men of integrity and honour.'

He began to sweat. He felt his fingers tremble on the shot-gun. He started to move it to bear on the rope, but the words echoing in his mind seemed to have an opposing force physically pushing against his gun. 'A civilized country must have laws … I swear to uphold the laws … integrity and honour.'

The judge was nearly finished. It was time. There was no more time to ponder the matter. It was time for action. It was now or never. The woman he loved would die in minutes if he did not act.

He looked up at Ann again. Her eyes were fixed wildly upon him. She knew her time was about to run out unless he acted.

He looked at Marshal Hansen. He saw the lines of pain etched in the man's face, and knew exactly what he was feeling. The fact that he was going to have to kill him too sent a sudden twinge through Levi, jerking his eyes back to meet the frantic eyes of his lover.

The judge nodded to the deputy standing at the rear of Ann's horse. Without hesitation he brought his hand down smartly on the animal's rump. The startled horse lunged forward, jerking out from under its rider, leaving her dangling at the end of the suspended rope.

Ann's legs made a frantic effort to grip the saddle as the horse lunged. The added jerk yanked the rope around her neck with a greater tightness than her own weight could have done. When her legs jerked free of the fleeing horse she kicked about wildly, frantically searching for something beneath her feet to lift the weight of her body. Her hands, bound behind her now, pulled wildly against the bonds, striving to get loose to grasp the strangling fetter.

Her face began to turn dark. The frantic spark in her eyes began to fade. Her kicking slowed. Her eyes rolled upward, out of focus. Her mouth, gaping wide, kept working as though trying to suck some breath of life-sustaining air past the barrier of her constricted throat, but finding nothing to ease its merciless grip.

Her jerking subsided to twitches, then to stillness. Her body swung back and forth slowly as the momentum of her thrashing was spent. There was no sound. There was no breath of wind. There was no noise of earth or sky. It was as if the collected mass of people were holding their breath with her, waiting for death to take them as well.

'No!' the anguished wail, ripped from the throat of Dusty Brickner shattered the unearthy silence. 'NO! NOOoooo!' His cry turned into a wail of despair and echoed down the valley of Ten Sleep Creek like the keening of a lost Banshee. He dropped to his knees in the road and buried his face in his hands, sobbing uncontrollably.

The sobbing of Kate Banner was joined by a sudden sob of unison, torn from a dozen other throats. The choking murmur of the crowd softly grew, mounting up to a dirge that lamented the terrible price of justice.

The door of the marshal's office opened cautiously. The sound had been so slight as to be almost unheard. If Marshal Hansen had been able to sleep, he never would have heard it.

There was nobody there. He looked about carefully, then started to close the door. Glancing down at the ground he grunted. Slowly he bent over and picked two pieces of metal shining softly in the first light of dawn. One was a Washakie County Deputy Sheriff badge. The other was the badge of a Pinkerton Range Detective.

The marshal sighed heavily. He looked once more at the faint dust in the air along the road leading out of town. He looked at the badges in his hand, shut his hand thoughtfully around them, and slowly closed the door.